MW00399740

BOOKS BY TIM MCBAIN & L.T. VARGUS
*Casting Shadows Everywhere*
*Fade to Black (Awake in the Dark #1)*
*Bled White (Awake in the Dark #2)*
*Red on the Inside (Awake in the Dark #3)*
*Back in Black (Awake in the Dark #4)*
*Beyond the Blue (Awake in the Dark #5)*
*The Scattered and the Dead Series*
*The Clowns*

# THE CLOWNS

# THE
# CLOWNS

TIM MCBAIN & L.T. VARGUS

COPYRIGHT © 2016 TIM MCBAIN & L.T. VARGUS

SMARMY PRESS

ALL RIGHTS RESERVED.


THIS IS A WORK OF FICTION. NAMES, CHARACTERS, BUSINESSES, PLACES, EVENTS AND INCIDENTS ARE EITHER THE PRODUCTS OF THE AUTHOR'S IMAGINATION OR USED IN A FICTITIOUS MANNER. ANY RESEMBLANCE TO ACTUAL PERSONS, LIVING OR DEAD, OR ACTUAL EVENTS IS PURELY COINCIDENTAL.

# THE CLOWNS

# CHAPTER ONE

October 28th
11:21 PM

The last swig tasted like piss. It always did. Rick tossed the empty, the aluminum tube scraping over the sidewalk. He tried to kick it and missed.

Whatever.

He walked on. He had other things on his mind, such as what a goddamn tease Chloe was. He couldn't believe it. It wasn't right, getting a guy all worked up like that for no good reason.

He lit a cigarette, slowing his gait a moment, smoke flitting into his left eye to make his eyelid scrunch up. He took a big drag, held it for a beat, exhaled smoke.

He thought maybe he'd go over to Chloe's tomorrow morning, try to finish the deed. What did they call it? Consummate the relationship? But then he remembered that she had school. She was sixteen. He was twenty.

Whatever.

His tattered Sex Pistols t-shirt was no match for the chill in the October air, especially since he'd removed the sleeves so his tattoo would be visible. A skull wearing a top hat adorned his shoulder. It was smoking a blunt. He got it for free at a party, and it had the haggard look of a prison tat. He couldn't remember whether the top hat had been his idea or

1

not. He'd been quite drunk.

Most people probably thought it was a legit prison tattoo, and he was fine with that. Everyone around here thought he was a hard ass ever since he knifed a kid outside of a punk show. It was in the alley behind the corner bar. He didn't like the way the kid was looking at him and went to slash his arm, but the kid moved and he sliced open his belly. Any deeper and some guts might have come spilling out, but no. It was just a spurt of blood. Just a flesh wound.

He spent two nights in jail, but he wasn't charged. The kid wouldn't cooperate with the police at all. No one around here would.

The violence cemented his reputation, though. It made him a known figure in the local punk scene. They started calling him Rick Dagger, fearing and revering him. The infamy even attracted girls, namely young, troubled ones. Most of them were big ol' hippos and butterfaces as it happened, but not Chloe. She was hot. Too bad she was such a goddamn tease.

He needed more beer. A 22 oz. of Steel Reserve. That'd keep him warm for a little while. He had change stashed in the hiding spot back at his place but no money on him. Quite a walk, but whatever.

Panhandling paid for the beers. He liked to say that panhandling paid the bills, but it wasn't true, technically. He had no bills. He lived in a squat, an abandoned house, with other vagrants. He scraped out enough to stay drunk and have cigarettes most all of the time. Sometimes there was enough to eat, too.

It had been this way for four years now. No school. No

family. No rules. Just beers and shows and the occasional fisticuffs. He was surprised, sometimes, that he still had all of his teeth.

Before all of this, before his violent reputation took shape here in the city, he'd been a nerd. Worse than a nerd. Back in the suburbs, he'd been a laughingstock, an object of ridicule. It was bad enough before they started calling him SBI. He was nothing. A scrawny nobody from the trailer park with the physique of Jack Skellington. Then he got caught looking at tranny porn and made fun of mercilessly.

He didn't know why he did it. He liked girls. There was something confusing about that blend of feminine and masculine, maybe. Something a little wrong. Something that embarrassed him terribly when the others found out. And they did. They all did. Word spread throughout the school.

SBI - Shemale Body Inspector. SBI agent Rick. Slick Rick likes chicks with dicks.

Lighthearted snickers led to taunts led to outright bullying. He got jumped in the parking lot next to the school, stomped by three big football players. Three cracked ribs and a broken nose that was still crooked to this day.

He quit school and moved to the city. He got so drunk that he fell asleep in the park those first few nights. Sprawled on a bench like some worthless bum, which he guessed he was.

Worse than no one.

Nobody knew him here, though. Didn't know about SBI. Didn't know about the chicks with dicks. They didn't know anything at all, and in that way he was free.

So he became someone new.

He started spiking his hair, stealing punk rock t-shirts from other squatters. He panhandled enough to stay drunk and high most of the time.

No responsibilities. No problems.

Then he started picking on people – pushing them, punching them. Kids at shows and on the streets got bruises and bloody noses to remember him by. Better to be the bully than the victim, he figured. There was a natural advantage to always being on the attack, always being on the prowl. Like a shark that never stopped swimming, never stopped hunting its next victim. You could tilt all things in life your way if you stayed on the offensive.

He flicked his cigarette butt into the curb where it exploded into a spray of sparks, and he lit another. Home was only a couple of blocks off now.

He cut through a wooded path behind some apartment complexes. Mud filled the wedges and fissures where the asphalt had pulled apart, and he felt the soft spaces squish under his shoes.

Something rattled nearby, startling him badly enough that his shoulders quivered and goose bumps plumped upon the flesh of his arms. He knew the noise, the metallic sound of the chain-link fence shaking against the post. It was loud. Too loud to be caused by the wind. The quaking stopped as his eyes drifted toward the fence.

He snapped his neck around to look up and down the length of the chain-link barrier. Nothing moved, and it was hard to make out much in the dim glow from the streetlights glinting through the tree branches. All tree trunk shadows and dark shapes, one blob impossible to discern from the

4

next.

The fence shivered again, a single violent shake that rang out for a long moment in the silence, and then there was a deeper sound. A laugh. A cartoonish, over the top cackle, but with a thick baritone that seemed out of place, made him uneasy.

Somehow his eyes knew where to look this time. They followed the noise to its source.

A man.

No.

A clown.

He could just make out the silhouette of the pointed hat atop the curly wig. The streetlights shined through the frizz of the hair enough that he could make out its orange hue, and for a moment he was reminded of the guy from Nickelback and his wavy mane.

A clown. A Nickelback clown. Maybe that wasn't so scary, especially since he must be on the other side of the fence. Rick took a breath.

But it wasn't on the other side of the fence.

The figure stepped forward, its laugh trailing off as it moved into a wedge of light along the edge of the asphalt. It stopped there, about ten feet from where Rick stood.

Rick wanted to backpedal, at least, if not sprint away, but he just stood, staring, his mouth open wide. The thin adhesive of saliva was the only thing keeping his cigarette connected to his bottom lip.

Red makeup smeared around the clown's wet mouth. It looked sloppy, the lines jagged and haphazard in a manner that seemed to suggest they were applied with aggression.

Roughly. Violently. The red stood out against the stark white makeup of the face. It was hard not to think of blood.

Rick swallowed in a dry throat, his Adam's apple bobbing. His body went rigid, blood rushing to his core, a panicked animal response that left him lightheaded, neon pink splotches blotting his vision. He had to focus to keep from fainting, forcing himself to take slow even breaths until his head cleared a little.

Laughing earlier or no, this wasn't a happy clown. The makeup etched a smile onto the face, but the lips themselves stayed flat for the moment, the brow scrunched as though annoyed.

The thing held so still that, for a second, Rick considered the notion that it may be a mask, but the clown blinked just then to shatter that thought just as it arrived. He realized that the eyes were opened too wide. Far too wide.

He broke eye contact then, his gaze swinging down to the oversized shoes. Unfastening his eyes from the clown's seemed to unfreeze his body, and he stutter-stepped back a couple of paces.

So yeah. He should get going.

Something struck him in the back of the head before he could turn to run. A blunt object that connected with a metallic ping and knocked him over all at once, the side of his head bashing into the blacktop before he could make any attempt at catching himself.

So that was confusing.

He recognized the sound right away, though. He'd heard it once as a kid playing baseball when Tyler Gutowski whacked the catcher, Wes Stump, in the head with an aluminum bat. It had been an accident. Probably. Anyway, that kind of sound sticks with a person, he supposed – aluminum against cranium.

He couldn't quite think straight from the blow, so he walked himself through the scenario: He lay on the ground, flat on his back, fingernails scraping at the asphalt as though to verify its reality.

Yep. It was real. Good to know.

But wait. What was he thinking about just before this? Something important. Baseball, right? No, before that.

Oh, right. The clown. Yeah. Yeah, he should get going.

He opened his eyes to find three clowns standing over him, one holding the aluminum bat, the others wielding knives. He didn't realize that another kneeled just next to him until he felt the sharp pain in his left wrist. Teeth dug into the flesh there, piercing little stones with the wet flap of lips circled around them.

He screamed then, and they were all on him. Stabbing. Biting. Opening him up in any way they could.

He thrashed. He kicked and flailed, succeeding in shaking one or two off at a time, but he couldn't pry free of all of them. Couldn't get free.

The blades penetrated his middle over and over. Invasions. Intrusions. The hard metal made him seem so soft.

And the cold, October air touched the wounds, reaching inside the newly fashioned crevices torn into his skin. The wet red drained out of him, the warmth of his insides sliding over the places going chilly, not enough to keep them warm.

When the clowns leaned their heads back and laughed, he felt just like how he used to feel, who he used to be.

The clowns fed, but they weren't sated. Not even close.

# CHAPTER TWO

October 28th
11:32 PM

The thud of Chloe's black combat boots kept a steady beat as she made her way down the street.

What an asshole, she thought, thinking back on her night with Rick.

She looked back over her shoulder at the playground where they'd parted ways. The top of the rusty slide was just visible from here. And next to it, the pointed nose of the jungle gym shaped like a rocketship. In a few steps both would be out of sight. She didn't know why she kept coming back. Or maybe she did, but she just didn't want to admit it.

Rick was a scumbag. She did know that. He was twenty. A high school drop out. He had some story about getting kicked out of the Marines, but she was pretty sure that was bullshit. She tried to imagine Rick with a crew cut, in an army uniform, and a chuckle escaped from her lips. Rick, in the military? Fat chance.

She popped her earbuds into her ears and then plugged the jack into her phone, but when she tried to turn it on, the low battery warning blinked at her.

"Damn it," she muttered. Stupid Rick and his filthy squat with no electricity. Fucking bums.

Coiling the cord of the headphones around the phone, she

shoved the whole mess back into her bag and continued her walk in silence.

Rick's last girlfriend – not that Chloe considered herself his girlfriend – had been thirteen, according to Gina Malone. An eighth grader for Christ's sake. Chloe's mouth actually puckered in distaste. There was also a rumor that he'd gotten her pregnant and then made her get an abortion, but she didn't know if that was true. This town liked to gossip, and she knew firsthand that most of it was bullshit.

OK, she'd established that Rick was a fucking loser from Planet Dickweed. So why did she keep going back?

She patted around in her jacket pockets for the pack of cigarettes she'd swiped from Rick's bag. She had other ways of getting them, but they tasted better when they were stolen. She pulled the lighter out – also Rick's – and lit the cigarette.

She had the same feeling she always had when she left Rick's place. A sort of sick feeling in the pit of her stomach. A mixture of dread and shame and confusion.

She took a long drag off the cigarette, held it in for a moment, relishing the burn and the tingle of the nicotine-laced smoke in her lungs. Smoke coiled out of her nostrils as she exhaled.

OK, so maybe she liked the attention she got from him. Maybe she liked feeling wanted. Desired. It was exhilarating and exciting when they were kissing and touching, and she could feel how much he wanted her. It started as an almost ticklish sensation in her stomach, and then a warmth would spread through her whole body, and her head would feel light, almost like she had a beer buzz, but better than that. In those moments, the world seemed simpler. Easier. Like nothing else mattered but their hands and lips and bodies. Nothing else mattered but the moment they were in. There was no past and no future. There was only the Now.

And yet... whenever it ended, the second she was alone again and left with her own thoughts, it was like she stepped off the edge of a cliff and plunged into a chasm of shitty feelings.

She flicked the cigarette with the tip of her thumb, knocking the cherry off the end.

Something always ruined the moment, of course. Tonight, for instance, they'd been making out in the mildewy La-Z-boy someone had dragged in off the street on bulk trash day. One of Rick's "roommates" wandered into the room while they were in the middle of it and just started vomiting. He wasn't quiet about it, either. He really heaved, and what seemed like buckets of orange-colored puke splashed onto the matted brown carpet.

Rick scrambled out of the recliner and onto his feet, nearly knocking Chloe onto the floor.

"Jesus, Malcolm!" Rick yelled.

When Malcolm finished, he casually wiped at the corner of his mouth with a sleeve, gave them a slow smile, and said, "Sorry, man. I didn't know anyone was in here."

Dirtball junkies.

A sigh had puffed out of Rick's nostrils, and without looking at her, he took Chloe by the wrist and led her out of the house to the playground down the street. He sat down on a merry-go-round with peeling red paint and tried to pull her down onto his lap. To continue where they'd left off, she guessed.

"Uh, sorry," she said, pulling her hand away. "But I'm kinda not in the mood anymore."

Usually he'd try to play it cool when she stopped him, making a joke about how she was giving him blue balls. But tonight... tonight he didn't make any jokes, and she had a fleeting thought, a momentary sense that she might be playing with fire. That maybe one of these nights, he wouldn't feel like stopping.

"Fine. Whatever," he said, then sneered. "You better get home, anyway. Wouldn't want you out late on a school night."

He liked to tease her like that, throw it in her face that she was still in high school. Like it made her lame somehow. She always wanted to ask, "If I'm so lame for still being in high school, then what does that make you for wanting to screw me?"

But she never did. For some reason, she had the sense that it would actually hurt his feelings, and she wasn't a total bitch.

They hadn't. Screwed, that is. Chloe was a virgin, which would have shocked probably just about everyone. Maybe even that asshole Rick, who hadn't even offered to walk her home. Not that she would have let him.

The wind kicked up, catching the dried leaves and some torn bits of trash and paper on the ground and spiraling them into a miniature tornado.

Chloe forgot the cigarette for a few paces and took a deep breath of the autumn air. She liked this time of year best. It felt like being on the cusp of something important. Every day there was some small change that edged them closer to winter. Last week, some of the leaves on the trees had still been green. Now they were almost all yellow turning to red.

A scraping, grating sound startled her from her thoughts. It sounded like metal being dragged over concrete or brick and came from somewhere behind her.

She did not stop walking. When you heard strange sounds in the city, it was best to keep moving. Especially if you were a girl.

She tried to speed up her pace without being obvious.

A low brick building ran along the street to her left. Mismatched blobs of brick-colored paint adorned the walls. Evidence of many attempts at covering graffiti. It gave the building a patchwork appearance.

When she came to the narrow alley at the edge of the building, she heard it again. That scraping sound. But this time, it came from down the alleyway. That wasn't right. The noise had definitely come from behind her before. It didn't make sense unless... unless someone was following her.

Her eyes strayed past a line of weeds growing from a crack in the pavement. The orange glow of the streetlights did not penetrate the darkness between the two buildings, and she squinted into the gloom.

It stepped out from the shadows, as if propelled forward by her gaze.

It was a clown.

She stopped, her feet suddenly rooted to the sidewalk as if she were one of the rogue dandelions sprouting up from the concrete.

The red and yellow outfit, painted face, and tufts of brightly colored hair might be cheery and fun to some people, but not Chloe.

Chloe hated clowns.

And then the metallic screech came again, and her eyes fell to the clown's waist, where a white-gloved hand clutched a machete and slid it over the brick exterior.

Chloe gasped and stepped back into the street, and then she was surrounded by bright lights and a car horn blared in her ears.

Tires screeched against the pavement. The car managed to swerve around her at the last second, and the driver yelled out the open window as he passed.

"Move, ya dumb bitch!"

The rumble of the muffler receded as the car continued on its way.

"Screw you, asswipe!" she yelled back, on instinct.

Chloe took a shaky breath, high on adrenaline after her near-collision with the car. It was a moment before she remembered what had startled her into the road in the first place.

Her head whipped back to the alleyway, but it was empty.

She shivered, thinking of the painted face and the blade. What the hell? What kind of psycho walks around dressed like a clown, carrying a machete? Just to scare people or what?

By the time she was walking up the front steps of her house, she had started to doubt the whole thing. Maybe the cigarettes she'd stolen from Rick were laced with something. That was a thing, right? Though she hadn't ever seen him do anything harder than pot or booze. He didn't have the funds, for one thing.

She tried the door. Locked. Dickheads. She dug around until she found her keys, which took a while because no one had left the porch light on, either. Mega-dickheads. She gave up, lifted the faux rock hide-a-key from next to a shriveled pot of neglected begonias, and unlocked the door.

She checked her breath in the palm of her hand as she slipped through the front door. It reeked of smoke. Most kids would carry around a pack of gum or a mini-bottle of Scope to try to cover their tracks. Chloe never bothered to cover her tracks. She didn't need to. Neither of her parents noticed anything she did.

Well, that wasn't totally true. Every few months her mom would decide something had crossed the line enough to warrant a grounding. Last time it was Chloe's nose ring. The funny thing was, she'd had it for almost a month before her mom even noticed.

Chloe supposed maybe they were under the impression that this was "a phase" that she'd grow out of eventually. That if they made too much of a stink, they'd only make it worse. Most times she figured they really didn't give a shit and had given their daughter up as a lost cause.

The TV was blaring from down the hall in her parents' room. The green neon glow of the digital clock on the microwave in the kitchen told her it was almost midnight. On a school night. No one had waited up for her. Typical. She wondered what would happen if she just didn't come home one of these nights. Would they even notice?

She swung the door of the fridge open wide, squinting into the light that seemed impossibly bright after being outside in the dark. Her stomach churned and growled. She hadn't eaten anything since school got out, when she grabbed a medium fry from McDonald's on the way to Rick's. Rick never had any food, so she hadn't even had a snack since three o'clock, let alone dinner.

She shifted the various bottles and jars and containers of leftovers around on the shelves before she settled on a peanut butter and jelly sandwich. She grabbed the jar of strawberry jam and let the fridge door close on its own.

Balancing two sandwiches on top of a glass of Sunny-D, she stomped up the stairs to her room.

She closed the door and locked it behind her. Her parents rarely bothered coming to her room these days, but when they did, it always pissed her mom off if the door was locked. Chloe always made sure it was.

Ignoring the light switch next to the door, she stooped and plugged in the strand of multi-color Christmas lights. They gave the room more ambiance than the overhead lighting, Chloe thought.

She lay back on her bed, paper plate resting on her belly while she took alternating bites of sandwich and swigs of Sunny-D. A glob of jelly dribbled out from between the bread, and she paused to lick it from her finger.

She remembered the guy in the clown suit again and shuddered. She hated clowns. Always had.

When she was little, her grandparents gave her a giant doll as a Christmas gift. Or tried to give it to her, anyway. It had red yarn hair and a painted face, with blue stars on the cheeks and big red lips. She screeched at the sight of it, and they had to put it out in the garage to get her to calm down. The doll was huge, bigger than Chloe at the age of three, and they thought maybe it was the size that frightened her. So they waited until she was five and tried again. Same reaction.

# The Clowns

Chloe didn't actually remember this, of course. But she'd heard her parents and grandparents rehash the story enough times that it almost felt like she did. And there were pictures. Photographs of a smaller, red-faced Chloe, wailing at the big, hideous clown monstrosity. Really, she didn't even know who would think that would be a good gift for a child. Why do adults think kids like clowns? Clowns were so goddamn creepy with those fake grins always plastered on their faces. No one smiles that much.

Chloe started to doze off then, still fully dressed, boots and all. She'd been asleep for a while when something caused her to stir. Not fully awake yet, she rolled over, eyes still closed. What was it?

Her throat was dry, mouth sticky from sleep. Right. She was thirsty.

Without opening her eyes, she flung out an arm, searching for the glass of Sunny-D. Her hand connected with something, and she had the sense of the room growing darker, even though her eyes were closed. She must have knocked the plug for the Christmas lights out of the socket. Oh well. Her hand resumed the errant search for the glass of juice.

And then she heard it.

A tapping sound. Coming from her window.

Someone was outside her bedroom window.

Her eyes snapped open, and her roving hand forgot about the Sunny-D.

Her room was dark, silent. She held her breath in the pitch black, waiting. Had she imagined it?

No, there it was again.

*Tap tap tap.*

Before the thought came to her all the way, she tried to stop it. Knew it was coming. Anticipated it. But it was too late.

She thought of the clown she'd seen earlier in the night, and icy fear crept up her spine.

The whole house was quiet now. Her parents had turned off their TV and gone to bed. She wanted to call out to them the way she had when she was little and had a nightmare. But she knew she couldn't. Or wouldn't.

The tapping continued, and Chloe held absolutely still. Maybe whoever it was would go away if she didn't make a sound. But then she remembered that she'd fallen asleep with the venetian blinds down but open and the Christmas lights on. They'd probably seen her lying there in bed. They weren't going to leave. They knew she was there.

The tapping came again and it suddenly occurred to her that it was probably Rick.

Yes, of course it was Rick. He was the only person stupid enough to come and knock on her bedroom window at night. He'd probably gotten into a fight with one of his squat-mates again and decided to leave until it blew over.

This was so Rick. He was probably just horny, and it was all a ruse to try to get into her room and then into her bed.

Really, did he think she was that dumb? Her parents were downstairs, for Christ's sake.

All her fear had vanished, and she scooted off the bed. Rick would be lucky if she didn't shove him off the roof.

At the window, she shoved the blinds aside and found... nothing.

No Rick. No nobody.

Maybe that should have made her feel better. It didn't. She tried to swallow again, but her mouth was so dry, there was nothing to swallow. She took a step backward and the movement reminded her of the way she'd stumbled into the street when she'd seen the clown, and the hair on her arms stood on end.

*Tap tap tap.*

She almost screamed when the tapping returned, but just as quickly her fear turned to anger again. Whoever it was, they were about to regret messing with her.

Chloe batted the blinds out of her way, unlatched the lock, and slid the window up. She thrust her head out the window, intending to look to either side where she figured Rick or whatever joker was out there was hiding. Instead, she came face to face with a pair of golden eyes.

The black cat trilled softly and leapt through the open window and into the room.

"Binky!" Chloe closed and locked the window, then stooped to lift the cat in her arms.

"You scared the crap out of me."

The cat purred as Chloe scratched under its chin and give it an affectionate squeeze.

She stumbled back to her bed and felt around in the dark until she found the end of the string of Christmas lights. Under the festive glow, she changed into her pajamas. She found the glass of Sunny-D and polished it off.

The guy in the clown suit had probably gotten a good laugh when she stumbled into the road like that. What wasn't so funny was her almost getting hit by a damn car. The angered returned. Well, whoever it was, if he kept it up, it was only a matter of time before he crossed the wrong person and got the shit kicked out of his polka dot ass.

On most nights, before she crawled into bed for good, she unplugged the Christmas lights. Not tonight. Tonight she left them on. It wasn't because she was still scared, though.

She left the lights on for the ambiance.

# CHAPTER THREE

October 29th
8:11 AM

Phillip Burkholder was late for art class. Again. It was his second tardy of the semester, and he was livid with himself, even if his excuse was a legitimate one.

"You saw what?" Mrs. Berman said.

"Clowns," Burkholder said. "Five of them."

"Clowns. In the woods outside of your apartment building. And this led to you being late for what reason?"

"The clowns were armed, ma'am. Well, one of them had a knife, at least."

"I see. And it was the blade that prevented you from making your way to school."

"Well, I had to call the police, of course. It was my civic duty."

"Right. I'm sure that's the case. Well, it looks like I'm out of questions. Maybe take a seat and get to work on your mosaic."

Phillip made his way to his seat, all eyes in the room on him. He still felt the chill of the long walk he'd just finished due to missing the bus, but the cold he felt from the others in this room bothered him more. He tucked his chin, eyes aimed at the ground. As soon as he sat, the familiar voice rasped behind him.

"Hey, Turdholder."

Greg Moffit and his lackeys laughed like hyenas. Moffit was tiny for his age. Short and narrow-shouldered. Between his size and the bright red rubber bands on his braces, he could have passed for a seventh grader instead of a junior. He was also the meanest kid that Phillip knew.

"Are you fucking serious, bro? Clowns? Really? Only real clown is you, Turdholder, and an ass clown at that."

More laughter. Phillip wanted to tell them to watch the Channel 7 news tonight and see how hard they were laughing when all of the facts came out. These clowns were real. They'd see.

He couldn't say anything, of course. He pretended he hadn't heard. Ignoring them was the only thing that sometimes worked.

Phillip was like a possum playing dead and Greg Moffit was a bear, snuffling at him. No, not a bear, he thought, remembering Greg's laugh. A hyena.

Something warm and wet hit the back of Phillip's neck. Spitballs. Again. Great.

Play dead, Phillip told himself. Play dead.

He wondered if there was a handbook or something out there made for high school bullies, filled with tips and tricks of the trade. How else did they all know the same old shenanigans?

Chapter one: Saliva based weaponry: Mastering spitballs, loogies, and wet willies.

Chapter two: The art of the taunt: Bastardize someone's name into something humiliating in minutes.

Chapter three: Going nuclear: Everything you wanted to

know about wedgies but were scared to ask.

"Turdholder. I'm fuckin' talking to you. Is it true what I heard?" Moffit said, pausing to snicker. "That your mom is some kind of big gross fatty?"

Phillip gripped his pencil harder, knuckles standing out white. Just play dead.

The voice spoke up from behind him:

"Hey, maybe you could just send your mom out there to eat the clowns, right? Has a certain logic to it, I think. Perhaps that would be her... what did you call it... civic duty."

Phillip's eyes clenched closed, eyelids and nose puckering into wrinkled wads of skin. Something inside of him snapped, and he whirled on Greg Moffit and his gaggle of laughing idiots.

"She has a medical condition, you imbecile!"

Greg Moffit's face froze, eyes wide, and for a minute, Phillip thought he had done it, that he'd finally shut him up.

And then Moffit turned to one of his friends, and they both howled with laughter.

"Imbecile? Is this motherfucker serious?" Moffit could barely get the words out, he was laughing so hard. "Who the hell talks like that?"

"Hey!" Mrs. Berman called from across the room. "More mosaic. Less chatter. What do I always say? W-W-W-dot-shutup-dot-com, right guys?"

The laughs didn't stop, not really, but they quieted some.

Phillip stood and walked across the room to the supply area, passing squeeze bottles of paint to locate the piles of construction paper and the jars full of scissors. He kept his head down as he selected a few colors of paper and reached into the jar to fish out the only pair of lefty scissors from the bottom. Their laughs seemed a little smaller now that he was some distance away, but they never fully went away.

He was silent, his face placid, but he screamed on the inside:

Fudge those guys. Fudge them in their fudging butts.

The rage made him grit his teeth, made his eyelids flutter of their own accord. Not things that anyone would notice from a distance, but they were there. He didn't think he was anywhere near tears. Not really. But he couldn't stop blinking. He took a deep breath before he turned and headed back for his table.

His eyes stayed on the floor as he walked into the hyenas' den. He never saw the figure off to the right who pushed him, though he knew upon impact that it must be one of Moffit's lackeys.

He flew, neck flinging back into a whiplash position, sheets of construction paper fluttering away from him in all directions. The scissors only stayed in his hand because his fingers were laced through the loops on the handle.

His arms spread out to the sides like wings, as though they could help him balance. It felt like he went fully horizontal in that moment, his face and belly and knees all facing the floor at a 90 degree angle even if that seemed impossible later.

He crashed into Moffit, knocking him out of his chair so they both tumbled to the floor. Phillip tried to bring his hands around to catch himself, and the opened scissors raked just in front of Moffit's face, coming just inches shy of his eyeballs.

Mrs. Berman looked up just in time to see what looked like an attempted scissor stabbing. She lurched to her feet, bellowing in a deep voice.

"Knock it off! Phillip! Out in the hall! Now!"

The room went silent as soon as she started yelling, that reverent quiet reserved for funerals and doctor's offices and awkward moments such as this. There seemed to be no movement apart from Mrs. Berman's heaving shoulders.

After a motionless beat, the boys disentangled and stood, both of them bowing their heads like shamed dogs, the scissors dropping to the floor between them. They stumbled away from each other, hands patting around them as though they were feeling their way along in the dark.

Phillip's lips parted, poised to explain the misunderstanding. He was pushed. Surely this could be cleared up.

"Not a word out of you, Phillip," Mrs. Berman said, the level of disgust in her voice hard to believe. "Forget the hallway. Go to the office. Now."

The murmurs picked up as he gathered his belongings from his desk, all of those whispering voices, hushed and tight. He could pick the hyena voices out of the pack.

"Did you see that, man?" Moffit said. "He fuckin' came right at me, tryin' to gouge my eyes out. Kid is fuckin' loco."

"He musta snapped, bro," another said.

And in a way Phillip wished that were the truth. If he were going to face the consequences, he may as well have really gone for it, right? Instead, he got bullied into trouble, the extent of his standing up for his mother's honor amounting to calling someone an imbecile, not even mustering a proper swear word, the kind of coarse language he would never use.

Light streamed through the windows in the principal's

25

office, reflecting off of the gleaming surface of the desk between Phillip and the school's ultimate authority figure. Mr. Hagen was a sallow-faced man with a puff of curly gray hair, but with the way he was backlit at the moment, Phillip mostly saw him in silhouette, a shadow with what looked like a Chia Pet on its head.

The man's voice had a deep resonance that juxtaposed with a fussy delivery that almost sounded like a fake British accent at times. It seemed like something that would be in a sitcom, one of the old ones.

"I'm willing to believe that you didn't intend to use the scissors as a weapon – and thank God no one got hurt – but I've got to take the teacher's word for it that you were the aggressor in this dispute, OK?"

Phillip shrugged. It smelled like cough drops in this room, the menthol ones with the over-the-top medicinal odor. It made Phillip's nostrils flare every so often, some subconscious attempt to clear them of the stench which never quite worked.

"The story doesn't really add up, though, does it? There's more to it, I expect. Some ongoing conflict, if I'm right. Why don't you tell me what's really going on here?"

Phillip said nothing. He had been through all of this before. The best case scenario, if he were to snitch on Moffit and the others, would be a round of supervised mediation with one of the guidance counselors. He'd sit across from Moffit and the rest in uncomfortable silence, watching them smile and nod and play along with the adult suggestions right up until they got let off the leash, at which point Phillip would get it worse than before.

No thanks.

Even if they did punish Moffit – legitimately punish him – what would come of it? A detention? An in-school suspension? These things made no difference. If they really wanted to take punitive action, how about suspending him from a couple of soccer games? Or kicking him off the team? That would be a real punishment.

It was hopeless, though. Nothing good came from tattling, Phillip knew. The adults in the school, perhaps all adults, had this idea of what the world must be like, and they enforced the rules to cater to their idea rather than reality. From what Phillip could tell, they didn't care about reality at all beyond their idea of it. He thought maybe they simply couldn't see it.

"With the scissors involved, I probably should suspend you, you know…" the principal said.

Phillip gasped, the fingernails of each hand digging into the wooden arms of his chair like the talons of some bird of prey.

"But I believe detention better fits this particular crime. Your attendance has been impeccable, apart from the tardy this morning. Your grades aren't quite up to snuff. You're flunking geometry as I recall?"

"That's correct," Phillip said, nodding. "Possibly social studies as well."

A disturbed look passed over Mr. Hagen's face, but it receded quickly.

"I see. Well, you do show up, at least. I can reward that with a bit of leniency, I think. Don't make me regret it."

Phillip's heart thundered as the principal signed the sheet of paper and handed it over. Detention. It could have been worse, he knew. His four year streak of perfect attendance

27

could have been shattered just like that.

The significance of it tumbled in Phillip's head as he walked back to his locker. The close brush with suspension took his mind off of the clowns entirely.

# CHAPTER FOUR

October 29th
9:46 AM

Avery squatted by her kitty in the grass field outside the apartment complex, hands running up and down the length of the orange cat's spine, ruffling its fur. Such a tolerant cat, Avery's mother thought. Not many fur-balls would put up with the rough touch of an eleven-month-old's little ham fists. Wizard wasn't like most cats, though. He trusted people completely, and more than that, he loved the attention, the affection, circling back to brush his whiskers and lip against the plump little arm.

Drool spilled from the toddler's mouth, a string of spittle draining down the side of the cat's leg. Patty smiled, a single puff of laughter emitting from her nostrils. All of this was so cute. She needed pictures.

Her hands searched her pockets almost subconsciously, both jacket and pants, fingers not finding the rectangular bulk they expected. No phone. She must have left it inside.

Shoot. Missed opportunity.

Now the baby hugged at the back of the cat, opening her mouth to try to capture the tip of the tail in her toothless maw. She smiled as she waggled her head about like a dancing snake's, never quite able to catch up to that swishing tube of fur.

**29**

Damn it all.

Patty could already feel the Likes piling up on Instagram and Facebook, if she'd just brought the stupid phone. Her hand fished into her pocket once more. Still nothing, of course.

Posting pictures of the baby had become her primary hobby. She even thought, sometimes, that maybe he'd come back to her if he saw how beautiful their baby really was, if he saw how special and precious his little girl was. If he saw how this was meant to be.

She glanced back over her shoulder, looking up at the second story balcony outside of their unit, the spider plant hanging over the patio chairs. It wasn't so far. How long would it take? Ninety seconds? Maybe less. Probably less. Especially if she jogged.

She looked back at Avery and Wizard, the two of them occupied with each other entirely. She knew there'd be no harm in leaving the girl for just a minute. The baby couldn't string together enough steps to make it out to the street, and she knew all of the neighbors well enough. Good people. It was all elderly folks in this building aside from her and Avery.

She walked in reverse a few paces, almost testing things out, watching the baby, seeing if she lurched or cried or even noticed her mother drifting away. Nothing. The fleshy little arms squeezed the cat again, and he coiled around behind the child, brushing that same side of his face across her shoulder blades on his way around.

She turned and ran for it, fingers ripping open the glass door into the complex, her heart already thumping from the little thrill of this, even if she knew there was no real risk.

# The Clowns

As soon as Patty disappeared into the building, the voice called from the woods.

"Here kitty, kitty."

The cat and girl both fixed their gazes in that direction. Dry leaves crunched and twigs snapped and there was a visible stirring of plant life there along the edge of the woods, but the foliage was too thick to see who might be calling. The voice repeated itself, lifting into a falsetto this time.

"Here kitty, kitty, kitty."

The cat trotted that way, intrigued. The baby's brow rumpled a moment, wrinkles forming and smoothing all around it, and then she tottered along after her feline companion. She loved her kitty.

When the clown appeared there, a massive smile on his face, neither child nor animal flinched. They kept heading toward their destination. The painted face contorted to smile even harder.

The baby toppled into the grass about halfway there, falling far behind. She looked up in time to see the cat in the clown's hands, and something wasn't right. It wasn't right at all.

Avery knew the clown was hurting the orange cat. Kind of. She couldn't fully process the encounter unfolding before her, didn't understand the way the head was twisting, but based on the sounds Wizard was making, she knew enough to start crying. She did not, however, retreat.

She wheeled around to face the building, all of her being expecting to find her mama off to her left. But no. No mommy. No one at all.

She was alone. That fact scared her more than the clown

itself.

Her bottom lip trembled now, and the sobs that came out of her sent two tremors through her torso that seemed to rattle her along the axis of her spine. Then she went rigid. The cries were nearly silent. Fully panicked gasps that sounded more like wheezing breaths than crying.

She hugged her tiny arms to her chest, hunched her back in a pose of fear, and remained utterly motionless. Even when the clown closed on her, even when he scooped her up into his arms, she held very, very still.

Patty burst out of the glass door moments later, her chest heaving from the run up and down the steps, the phone gripped in her mitt. There. It was done. Quicker than she had figured, too, she thought.

But just when the ease of that tension began to settle over her, her eyes scanned the field, and her chest got all tight.

No Avery. No cat.

"Avery?" she called out, embarrassed right away by the naked fear she heard in her voice.

There was no answer. No sound at all but the hum of traffic in the distance.

She took a step forward, hesitated, took another. The arches of her feet balanced on the nub where the asphalt dead ended into the grass. Somehow crossing the threshold seemed to free her up to full mobility.

The cat lay near the edge of the woods. Motionless. She rushed to it, kneeled, touched it and found it as limp as a wet towel, already going a little cool. Wizard was dead.

She realized her mouth was open when the dry of the air touched her throat. Her bladder ached just then, and she could hear the blood beating through her ears. This couldn't be real. It was too awful to be real.

A breath scraped into her lungs when she saw it. The tiny forearm protruded from the tall grass where the woods began in earnest, the rest of the body concealed by the foliage. She watched that fleshy arm for a moment before the terror fully hit. It didn't move.

Panic blurred her thoughts, severing her from reality as she scooted over to where it lay. She scooped the bloody lump from the ground and examined it, her chest and neck constricted. An incredible amount of the flesh had been removed considering the time frame, revealing the sinew and stringy muscle fiber wiring the jaw to the cheek bones. She hugged it to her chest, squeezing it tighter as though that could stop it from feeling wrong, feeling too small, feeling skeletal. She ran then, some panicked animal response that lacked all reason. She ran and ran with no place to go, no destination in mind, screaming as she carried her dead baby out into the street.

# CHAPTER FIVE

October 29th
9:58 AM

Chloe lifted her head from the pillow, dimly aware of the alarm on her phone screeching its shrill cry at her. She pawed at it until it shut up. The clock next to her bed was just a blurred red blob in her half-awake state. Her eyes blinked open and shut slowly, trying to make the numbers come into focus.

9:58 AM.

Shit. School started hours ago. Had she really slept through her alarm clock for almost three hours?

She rolled out of bed, feeling groggy, like she hadn't slept well.

On her drive to school, she thought about Rick and asked herself again what she was doing with him.

If you stripped away the leather jacket and the spiked bracelets, wasn't he just like every other guy? Did she actually think Rick liked her for anything more than superficial reasons? For the things she thought and said and felt?

Chloe stomped into school, yawning. Just before she went through the double doors, she spat out the piece of mint gum she'd been chewing in lieu of brushing her teeth. The sticky wad of neon blue missed the garbage bin she'd been aiming at by over a foot, but she kept walking. She was already late for third hour.

The halls were mostly empty, but by some shitty twist of fate, she wound up passing Greg Moffit on her way to class.

"Hey! Oscar Mayer!"

Chloe flipped him the bird with both hands.

"Eat a dick, Greg."

Her luck reversed when she reached her classroom. Her biology teacher had his back to the class when Chloe slunk through the door, and he was so immersed in the diagram of cell structure he was outlining on the overhead projector, he didn't even notice she was late.

Chloe's mind drifted to thoughts of Rick. They didn't generally do much talking. Mostly they made out and went to shows. One of the few times they'd had an actual conversation, she remembered that Rick had started out by asking her if she was afraid of heights.

"I don't know," she said. "Maybe a little."

"'Cause you might fall?"

"Yeah, I guess," she said.

He'd gotten this cocky look on his face then, lips puckered into a little smile.

"Not me. I ain't afraid of fallin'."

She cocked an eyebrow, not sure where this was going. Was he trying to impress her with his fearlessness or what?

"Nah, fallin' ain't the scary part," he continued. "It's hittin' the ground. That's the part you should be worried about."

He'd taken a swig of his PBR tallboy then, obviously pleased with himself over this revelation. Before she could say anything else, he'd sucked the last of the beer from the can, tossed it in the corner of his dingy little room, and went back to groping her breasts.

Well, that's stupid, she thought. Falling and hitting the ground kind of went hand-in-hand in that scenario.

It occurred to her, as he slipped a probing tongue between her lips, that the whole conversation had seemed rehearsed. Like he'd said it all before. Like maybe he thought this little anecdote was so clever, so charming, that he trotted it out from time to time. Probably for whatever teenage girl he was currently trying to bone.

She imagined him practicing the conversation in the mirror, smoothing the sides of his mohawk as he tried out different turns of phrase. A breathy giggle escaped her mouth, and he pulled away.

"What's funny?"

Shit.

Not willing to admit that she'd been laughing at him, she wriggled a little, drawing attention to where he had his hands up her shirt.

"That tickles," she said, then put her hand on the back of his neck and pulled him into a kiss.

Now, as she listened to Mr. Dunton drone on about mitrochondria, Chloe was disgusted with herself. How could she let herself get dragged into these situations?

She'd been an early bloomer, developing a full set of breasts by the time she was in sixth grade, when most of the other girls were still wearing training bras.

The boys in her class dared each other to pretend to trip in front of her or sometimes pushed one another toward her, hoping to cop a feel when they put out their hands to purportedly catch themselves.

They snapped the straps of her bra in the hallway, in class, in the darkened auditorium when they had assemblies.

They had contests to see who could be the first to land a Skittle in her cleavage from across the room.

More than anything, though, she hated the way they stared at her. A few times she even caught some of the male teachers gazing at her chest.

Her mother was inexplicably proud of the attention Chloe drew from men. When they were at the mall once, she'd whispered conspiratorially as they headed for the Jamba Juice.

"Did you notice that guy?"

Chloe glanced around at the bustling shoppers in the food court. "What guy?"

"The one in Macy's that was more interested in checking out *your* rack than the one holding the clothes."

Chloe instinctively crossed her arms over her chest, covering herself.

"Mom! Gross!"

"I bet he thought you were at least sixteen." She said it like it was a good thing.

"He was older than dad," Chloe said, her nose wrinkling in distaste.

"Enjoy it," her mother said. "You won't have it forever."

Chloe shook her head, baffled. Whatever "it" was, she remembered hoping she lost it sooner rather than later.

She'd played soccer since second grade, and in sixth grade she joined the volleyball team, too. She was good at both, a mean striker on the field and a decent setter on the court. Her mother was pleased, having been an athletic, popular teen herself.

Chloe was at school one day, heading to class, when she passed a group of boys. Eighth graders. One turned to the others and made a crude gesture at his chest. Her face grew hot, knowing they were talking about her. She looked away and hurried down the hall. At her next volleyball game, there was a suspicious surge in attendance, most of the newcomers being boys from her school. Boys who had never shown even the slightest interest in girl's sports. She felt their eyes on her. Heard how they cheered extra loud when she made a lunge for the ball.

She hoped it was a one-time thing, but at the next game, there were more of them.

She started doubling up on her sports bras before games, trying to smush her large breasts into something smaller and less conspicuous. She switched back to one bra when she overheard one of the older girls on the team refer to her as Uniboob.

And so, she did her best to ignore it. During sports, she focused on the game, eyes never leaving the ball. If she didn't see them watching her, she could pretend they weren't there. During school, she focused on her school work, eyes on the chalkboard, ears only pricking up to hear what her teachers had to say. And in the hallway in between... well, she had her friends. If she noticed any giggling coming from the boys, she didn't show it. She'd turn to her best friend, Faith, and concentrate singularly on her complaints about her parents or her excitement for the upcoming school dance or her dread over her fifth hour math quiz. They'd been best friends since third grade, and they were inseparable.

Nearly every Friday, Chloe rode the bus home and stayed the night at Faith's house, or vice versa. She remembered one such sleepover, when Chloe noticed Faith watching her from the corner of her eyes as she changed into her pajamas.

Faith was sprawled belly-down on her bed, and she pushed her chin up with a fist.

"I wish I had big boobs like you."

Chloe scoffed. "No, you don't. I would trade anything to have normal boobs."

Faith stood and went to the mirror.

"At least you *have* boobs. I look like an eight-year-old boy."

Faith tried in vain to push her non-existent breasts into something resembling cleavage.

"Trust me, you're lucky that no one pays attention to you," Chloe said, then immediately realized how awful that sounded. "I mean- I didn't mean it like that, Faith!"

But it was too late, and she saw Faith's chin quiver as she struggled to hold back the tears.

Chloe vaulted over the bed and wrapped her arms around her friend.

"Greg doesn't even know my name!" Faith wailed. Faith had been in love with Greg Moffit since their first day of sixth grade. Chloe didn't personally see the appeal. His eyebrows connected in the middle and he had a tendency toward bullying. She hugged her friend tighter.

"I'm sorry, I really didn't mean it like that. I just meant that... sometimes the attention might seem nice, but it's not nice when you can't turn it off."

Faith sniffled.

"Besides," Chloe said, picking up the stuffed panda she'd given Faith for her birthday. "I bet Greg has a matching one of these named Faith."

Faith had named the stuffed panda Greg after her crush and snuggled with it every night before she fell asleep.

"He does not!"

Chloe nodded.

"Yeah, and every night he confesses his love for you." She gazed into the bear's shiny black button eyes. "Oh, Faith, my love! I can't bear to be without you any longer."

She pretended to furiously make out with the stuffed animal, and they both laughed.

The rest of it was forgotten. Or so Chloe thought.

The bell rang, signaling the end of third hour. Chloe shuffled to her locker and traded her five-ton biology textbook for a beat-up paperback of *Lord of the Flies.* As she slammed her locker shut, the box of Lemonheads that served as her breakfast fell from her hand. Tiny yellow candy balls spilled from the open end, bouncing and rolling over the tile floor.

"Shit!"

She dropped to her knees, trying to catch the candies before the Five Second Rule expired.

Noticing a pair of feet loitering nearby, she traced the legs upward to find Kyle O'Brien gazing down her shirt. She stood up, stepped closer, and hugged her arms to her sides to further emphasize her cleavage.

"Like what you see?" She'd perfected the throaty voice over the years. Just the perfect blend of sexy and menacing.

Kyle stumbled backward, like if she got too close, he might catch some kind of infectious disease.

"Fucking dyke!"

She smiled to herself as he retreated. Pulling a small notebook from her bag, she flipped open to a page and drew a line under the heading, "Dyke." Next to that was a heading that read, "Slut" with more hash lines underneath.

"Ooh, and dyke pulls ahead by a nose," she said to herself.

Keeping track of the names she was called and the rumors that circulated was one of her hobbies. A little something to pass the time.

She was reviled as both a dyke and a slut by her classmates, which she had never figured out. While she was certain there were plenty of promiscuous lesbians and that the two weren't mutually exclusive, she knew the rumors. If the things the kids at school said about her were true, she'd blown half the senior class, had three abortions, and got caught giving Mr. Barnes a handjob during his prep hour.

Of course, none of the stories were true.

So far this month, she'd racked up an impressive eleven Dykes and ten Sluts. Naturally, her peers used a bit more variety than just those two terms. If she were called queer, faggot, carpetmuncher, or lesbotron, she counted it as a Dyke vote. Whore, skank, and human cum dumpster were filed under Slut. For a while she'd kept track of bitch, witch, freak, etc, under the heading "Misc," but Dyke and Slut always won out, so she'd let counting the rest fall by the wayside.

Rick was different in that way, at least. He didn't judge her or call her names. He wasn't superficial like most of the assholes she went to school with. And deep down, under the

Mr. Punk Rock exterior, she knew he wasn't really a tough guy. That lurking under the shellacked hair and bleach spattered t-shirts, he was vulnerable. Like her.

And despite her little performance with Kyle O'Brien, she would never actually allow a neanderthal like him to get within ten feet of her. She'd just learned that most guys freaked out if she responded to their leering like a psychotic nymphomaniac.

Maybe that was what she liked about Rick. Chloe had power over him. She *let* him touch her, and that gave her control. She knew somehow that despite the Rick Dagger act, he would never hurt her. He may have been twenty numerically, but underneath it all, she didn't think he had much more backbone than a high school freshman.

She slumped lower in her chair. Was that all it was about? Control? She was fooling herself after all. She didn't care about Rick, and he didn't care about her. She knew that. It was all a game of cat and mouse. She tried to tell herself that at least she was the cat in this situation, but she couldn't help think that maybe they were actually more like two dumb chickens, pecking at each other in a pathetic attempt to make themselves feel superior. A pointless and endless power struggle.

Chloe's daily ritual was to sneak her lunch under the B Hall stairwell. Eating there eliminated the need to find a non-hostile table in the cafeteria. There were people she could sit with, of course. Other outcasts and rejects. Nerds and dorks and even a handful of genuinely kind people who didn't judge her, or at the very least, pretended not to.

# The Clowns

But sitting in the cafeteria with the all of the sounds reflecting off the whitewashed cinderblock walls – trays slapping against tables, chairs scraping across floors, talking, shouting, laughing – always overwhelmed her. She felt like a zebra at a watering hole in the Sahara, too nervous to lower her head to drink for fear that a lion might sneak up behind her.

As her molars pulverized a mouthful of Chex mix, she overheard two girls talking in the hall.

"He said he saw a clown."

"Ew. What?"

Chloe's jaw froze mid-chew. Had she heard that right? Had the girl said *clown*?

"I know. That's what I said. Clowns are gross."

"Ew. So gross. But what was he doing?"

"Phillip Burkholder? Or the clown?"

Chloe set the Ziploc baggie of Chex mix on top of her paper lunch bag and crept closer to the girls, still concealed within the shadow of the stairwell.

"Ew. You didn't say it was Phillip Burkholder. He's gross."

"Yeah, I did, but you keep interrupting."

The two girls entered the bathroom across the hallway from Chloe's vantage point under the stairs. Their voices reverberated off the tiled walls, distorting and elongating their voices.

"Sorry! Well, what was the clown doing when Phillip saw him?"

"Just standing there, I guess. I mean, that's if you even believe him."

Shit. They were all the way in the bathroom now, and the

**43**

echo made it hard to understand what they were saying.

Chloe debated for a moment before deciding to go in after them. She had to hear the rest.

She strode into the bathroom, and the girls stopped chatting for a beat. But once they saw that it was just a nobody – just Chloe the Lesbian Slut-Witch – they went back to their conversation.

Chloe sidled into the handicapped stall and locked the door behind her. Being a nobody did have its perks sometimes. No one seemed to care if she overheard them, and she'd eavesdropped a lot of juicy nuggets over the years.

"Ew. But wait. You think he made it up?"

"I don't know. Probably. Who just walks around dressed up like a clown?"

Chloe held her breath, thinking of the clown she'd seen the night before. Who does that, indeed, she thought.

"Maybe it was someone from, like, a birthday party. When I was five, my mom got a clown for my birthday party. He did magic and made everyone balloon animals."

"Oh my god, that's hilarious." The girl snickered, as if a five-year-old having a clown-themed birthday party was the lamest thing she'd ever heard.

"I know. So gross."

Chloe remained cloistered in the stall even after the girls left, absorbed with what she'd heard.

The shriek of metal on brick – like a grown-up version of nails on a chalkboard – sounded in her memory, and then she saw it again in her mind's eye. The clown with his dead eyes and demented grin. It had been too dark and too great a distance to know for sure if the eyes were dead and the grin

**44**

was demented, but she just assumed.

What were the odds that she and Phillip had seen the same clown? Pretty high, she thought. It wasn't like there was a whole troop of deranged clowns randomly lurking around town.

And she knew why people were saying the kid made it up, too. If she hadn't seen it herself, she would have thought he was a loony, concocting stories for attention or something.

She had a vague idea of who Phillip Burkholder was. Enough to know that most people called him Turdholder. He was a nerd. One of those guys that may have hit puberty but was somehow still half a kid. He seemed like he might still watch Saturday morning cartoons and play with Lego blocks and let his mom pick out his clothes. Utterly at the mercy of jerk-offs like Greg Moffit.

She felt a small wave of relief. What she'd seen was real, that was confirmed. She wasn't seeing shit, and she wasn't insane.

Following the relief, she got a twinge of guilt that Phillip would get no such reprieve. She almost considered finding him between classes. Saying something. She felt bad, people talking about him like he was making it up. More fodder for the bullies. But she didn't stick her neck out. There was a reason she ate her lunch under the stairs. Chloe Trepper kept a low profile.

Some might argue that her dyed hair, eccentric clothes, and dramatic makeup were the opposite of a low profile. She thought of it more like being a poisonous snake or one of those tree frogs in the Amazon rainforest. Don't touch, her look said, or you might regret it.

She sighed. Poor Phillip. Kid needed to toughen up.

She tried to imagine him with a Rick Dagger costume on –
steel-toed boots, a few facial piercings, and a screen-printed
bum flap. She didn't think the guys at school would be so hot
to fuck with him then.

A memory came to her. The time they'd been at a show,
and Rick had bemoaned all the kids from the suburbs in
crusty attire.

"They're all posers, man. They don't actually need those
bum flaps."

"Need them?" she had asked.

"You think I wear this as a style choice?" He flicked the
Crass patch that was attached to his belt and hung over his
butt. "It's because I make my home on the streets. I don't
always have a cushy chair to sit in. It protects my pants from
getting too worn when I sit on the curbs and shit, man. It's
about a lifestyle."

Chloe had thought that was just about the stupidest thing
she'd ever heard. First, because she didn't see how some flimsy
scrap of cotton was going to protect his jeans. And second,
because it was absolutely, one-hundred percent a style choice.
Rick was so full of shit.

No. No, she would not get sucked into another why-am-I-
with-Rick vortex of confusion and misery. She didn't want to
think about him right now.

Her gaze wandered as she made her way down the
hallway. She turned a corner and there was Faith. Their eyes
met for a brief moment before Faith looked away. There was
not a trace of recognition in her eyes, which Chloe knew was
phony, but it hurt anyway.

One of Faith's new friends said something Chloe couldn't make out, and they all laughed. Even though she was pretty sure they hadn't been talking about her, to see Faith laughing and joking with her friends tweaked an old wound. She had not uttered so much as a syllable to Chloe in over three years.

Chloe didn't generally admit it to herself, but she was lonely. The kids at school thought she was a freak. Even her parents seemed to want to keep her at arm's length. She had no siblings.

She slid into the chair closest to the door of her History class.

Aside from Rick, she had barely anyone to talk to.

Rick.

Oh god.

She let her head fall forward and hit the desk.

It was the first time it dawned on her that she was partially with him out of loneliness. That was the real reason she let him get close. Let him touch her and use her. She wasn't some powerful Amazonian goddess, toying with her subservient man-slave. She was bartering with him. Trading her body for something resembling affection.

Well, that was it then. She'd have to break it off with Rick.

The sooner the better, too. Before she lost her nerve. Today. After school. She'd go to the squat and tell him she couldn't see him anymore. Maybe she'd make up some story about her parents finding out about him. Her dad threatened to get out his shotgun and go after the scoundrel that was corrupting his young, delicate flower of a daughter.

She wasn't sure if that was more or less likely to keep Rick from poking around. Would he try to get her back? Would he even care? They weren't even really dating. She didn't think they were, anyway. He hadn't, like, asked her to be his girlfriend or anything.

She tried to imagine Rick getting down on one knee, sliding a promise ring onto her finger, and saying, with his voice wavering and full of emotion, "Chloe Trepper, will you be my girl?"

This got a little snort out of her, and Gretchen Peters, who sat in front of her, turned around and gave her a dirty look.

Chloe licked her lips salaciously and blew Gretchen a kiss. Gretchen whipped her head around, scoffing as if completely scandalized by the whole ordeal.

OK, so maybe she had an inkling of where the lesbian rumors came from. Really, the kids in this school were so gullible and easy to manipulate. It was pathetic.

Someday she'd get out of this place. Go somewhere exotic. Europe, maybe. She'd never been, but she had a sense that people were less judgmental there.

She suddenly wished Rick had a phone so she could break up with him via text. It was a total dick move, but she couldn't shake the worry that she'd get there and chicken out. He'd get that look in his eye, that total and complete hunger for her, and she'd get weak. God, what was wrong with her? How could she be so simultaneously attracted to and repulsed by someone?

# CHAPTER SIX

October 29th
5:29 PM

Moffit slid the latex mask over his face, the rubber flaps folding his ears on the way down. Christ, it already felt moist inside. Dank and sweaty. He exhaled and his breath blew back into his face. It smelled like Pringles. And ass.

"Well… How's it look?" he said, his voice muffled and strange.

"Looks good," Danny said, chuckling. "Holy shit. This is going to be hilarious."

Moffit turned his head, the edges of the eyeholes partially obscuring his friend's face. The red-haired kid swung into view, cords standing out in his neck as he grimaced and smiled at the same time. Moffit returned the smile, and his taut cheeks pressed balls of flesh into the latex.

"Does it look scary?"

"Uh, yeah. Creepy as hell. Jesus, dude. I can't believe we're doing this."

Moffit detected a hint of real doubt in Danny's voice and moved to snuff it out right away.

"Don't be a pussy. Turdholder has to pay. Piece of shit wants to lunge at me like that? Pair of scissors or whatever? Fuck that."

Danny nodded, lips pulling down to expose his teeth in a

**49**

grimace again, those cords reappearing on his throat.

"Try yours on."

Danny shook his mask a few times as though that might loosen it up, and he pulled it on. Moffit laughed. The initial flash was pretty creepy, he thought, but the baked-in expression killed the effect quickly.

"Damn," he said.

"What? You don't like it?" Danny said.

"It's a little stiff is all. Looks pretty fake. Out in the dark, in the shadows, I think it will work, though. Turdholder is a little bitch, you know? He'd be scared of Ronald McDonald."

They walked to the bathroom and looked at themselves in the mirror, two clown masks staring back at them. Moffit's was fairly low-key as far as creepy clown masks went. He looked like a normal clown with just the vaguest hint of aggression around the edges of the lips and brow.

Danny's mask was far more over the top. Stitched up gashes formed seams from the corners of the mouth up past the forehead, as though the mask were made of a real human face pulled apart and sewn back together. The chin and jowls sagged in a realistic manner, and the clown makeup was pretty understated – a painted on brow, a little blue around the eyes, and a brownish red ring around the mouth that Moffit thought looked the shade of dried blood. The rest of the face was plain white paint. Most creepy clown masks were angular and tight, but he liked the way this one was soft and saggy and incongruent. Flaps of skin that could just slide away.

Turning his attention back to his own visage, Moffit moved his jaw around to get a feel for the amount of articulation the mask gave him. Not much. Probably better to keep quiet and mostly motionless, anyway. More tension that way.

"Are we gonna… you know… beat… beat him up?" Danny said.

"What? No. We're gonna be laughing so hard once he pisses himself, you know? I doubt we'll be in a violent mood."

Danny laughed for a second.

"What do you think he saw?" the red-haired boy said. "For real, I mean. People dressed up or something?"

Moffit shrugged.

"How should I know? He sure as shit didn't see evil clowns, though. It's ridiculous."

Moffit pulled the bottom of his mask up to free his mouth, and the fresh air sucked into his lungs all cool and nice.

"Let's do this," he said, his voice sounding clear and bright for a change.

With the masks balled up under their arms, the boys trudged through the woods and the brush behind the apartment complex where Turdholder lived. It was subsidized housing, Moffit remembered his mother saying, though he didn't fully understand what that meant. He knew enough to know Turdholder was poor. Of course, everyone in this neighborhood was poor, Moffit and Danny included. But the people living in this apartment complex were the poorest of the poor, the way he understood it.

The dusk faded quickly to dark, and the shadows swelled up to fill in the spaces all around them with blackness. Trees and foliage swathed in gloom. The dead leaves rasped under their feet.

Moffit felt his pulse quicken, the blood slugging away in his neck. He felt that little twinge of electricity flare in his head, a fevered excitement that made his cheeks ache with the desire to laugh. It was a particular kind of pleasure that he only associated with small cruelties such as this. Scaring someone. Teasing someone. Knocking someone flat on their ass in soccer. The little humiliations that made life worth living.

When the apartment buildings got within viewing distance, Moffit crouched in the brush just along the edge of the woods, and Danny followed his friend's lead. They said nothing, just looking up at the glow of the apartment windows, most of them lit with the harsh shimmer of fluorescent bulbs. All of those shining rectangles with movement flitting around inside of their borders. It almost looked like a bank of TV screens, Moffit thought, like maybe this whole building existed for his amusement.

"Masks on," Moffit said, and they pulled them on.

Next he reached into the cargo bag at his side, and there was a metallic clatter before he pulled the knives free. They were dull steak knives, not very intimidating when it came to weapons. But in the dark, they would do. The streetlight caught the blade, and the metal glittered for a moment as he passed one to Danny.

"Have your phone at the ready, bro," he said. "You're the director and shit. If Turdholder pisses himself, and we don't get that up on YouTube pronto, it's you who will have to live with the eternal shame of missing that opportunity. Probably not worth it."

"Right. No pressure," Danny said, laughing.

They waited for a long while. The wind blew through the thicket, brushing floppy fern leaves at them and rattling dried out stalks of thistle.

Moffit's mind wandered as they crouched there in silence. He thought about his dad. The smell of the fallen pine needles they were sitting on made him remember the time they went on a camping trip when he was young, and his parents were still together. It was a blurry memory, smudged and smeared by the years gone by, but he remembered building a bonfire as the night crept in. He could still call to mind the picture of his dad hunched over the fire, the orange light flickering on his beard. It was the first time he'd ever had S'mores.

His father had canceled again as far as picking him up this weekend. The visits were supposed to be every other weekend, and they'd maintained that biweekly schedule for the first two years after the divorce. The regularity slipped as time wore on. Now it was more like every six or eight weeks. He'd done the math. That made it around seven times per year total. Fourteen days out of 365, not quite four percent. He knew it'd be less – that it'd be zero percent – if his dad didn't have to feel guilty about it.

The night air grew thicker as they sat there, and inside the mask, it was almost unbearably humid, a wet and warm that contrasted with the chill outside in a way that made Moffit a little queasy.

The wait continued.

# CHAPTER SEVEN

*October 29th*
*5:47 PM*

The police scanner blared when Phillip got home, as it often did. His mom loved that damn thing more than TV or movies or books. Distorted voices droned, nearly indecipherable, every exchange punctuated with an "over" or a "roger that."

He closed the door with great care to keep it quiet and set his bag down next to the door with a similar effort at soundlessness. Detention had kept him an extra 90 minutes after school, and he'd walked the long way home after that, not relishing the conversation that was sure to transpire when he finally got here. Maybe he'd get lucky, though. Maybe she had the police scanner up so loud that she wouldn't hear that he was home.

No luck. Her lilting voice called from the next room.

"Phillip?"

"Yeah."

"Come in here."

The stern edge was there in her tone. She didn't yell, or at least it was a very rare occasion. Her voice hardened, though. It solidified into something angry, something angular and mean. Sharp.

He stood in the doorway to her room, eyes aimed low. He

could see her, just barely, a blurry blob at the top of his field of vision. She was big. Very, very big. So far as Phillip knew, it'd been years since she left the bed. It'd been this way for so long, in fact, that he couldn't remember what things were like before very well, back when she was still ambulatory. She didn't talk about her medical problems much, but he knew enough to know that it was an untreatable glandular disorder that had done this to her, had imprisoned her in this bedroom.

"A detention? A tardy? That's quite a day, huh? I don't know what's gotten into you lately."

He said nothing, his fingers fidgeting a little.

"I know things aren't always easy for you. I wish so badly I could be the kind of mother that could take you to the zoo or to the arcade, but I just can't."

Though he remained silent, his lips tightened. Zoo? Arcade? It was like she thought he was seven years old.

"No PlayStation for two weeks," she said, that hard edge in her voice receding into breathy resignation. "Bring it to me."

He nodded and turned to go to his room. Again, those rapid blinks transpired, eyelids juddering up and down in fast motion. He didn't know if it was anger or sadness or frustration that caused them this time around. Maybe all of the above.

Kneeling, he un-snaked the wires from behind the bulk of the ancient TV and went to work wrapping them around the gun metal gray box, making everything neat and tidy. It was a PS1 he'd found at a garage sale. Old, but still fun.

He could try to tell her about what really happened, about

what Moffit and his friends were really like. But adults didn't want to hear these things. They could understand cruelty in the abstract, but they suddenly turned obtuse when confronted with the real thing. That sadistic glee some took in making others suffer, in power and control. It didn't fit how they wanted to see the world.

Plus, he didn't want to tell her that Moffit had insulted her. What had he called her? A "weird gross fatty" or something like that? What a penis that guy was. He hated to even think that kind of language, but there it was. Greg Moffit. Total penis.

She was his mother, and he would take all of the humiliation and embarrassment to protect her if he could. Let him be the one to see how cruel the world really was. Let him suffer to spare her from the awful truth as much as possible. She didn't know any better, he figured. Her life was a different experience from most altogether.

If anyone had the inkling to get to know her rather than judging her on sight, they would have found an exceptionally sweet person with an almost girlish voice and a high tinkling laugh. How she maintained her sense of humor, her good spirits, he never knew, but she always did. She never got down, or if she did, she didn't show it.

It seemed so unfair. Sometimes he lay in bed, so angry about it that he cursed God. Why? Why make a world as dumb and mean-spirited as this? What for?

He carried the box with the wires wrapped around it into his mother's room. She pointed, hand bouncing on a pudgy wrist.

"In the closet," she said.

The Clowns

The closet door slid open. He stooped and nestled the PlayStation among all the shoes she hadn't touched in years.

"I love you, mom," he said, his back still to her, and then he turned to look at her.

"I love you, too," she said, and she smiled, but her eyes were far away, her attention occupied by those walkie-talkie voices spilling endlessly out of the speakers.

Out in the kitchen he fixed himself some dinner, his usual meal – a box of off-brand mac and cheese, which he seasoned with spurts of ketchup now and then. Before taking the first bite, he bowed his head. There was a long beat of silence before he muttered an, "Amen." The noodles squished when he took the fork to the bowl, a noise he originally thought was kind of gross and had grown to find great comfort in as this process became a ritual.

After dinner, he sat before the TV, fidgeting with the RCA rabbit ears he'd bought from Radio Shack for $8. Channel 7 cut in and out a few times, the picture flashing to a black screen that said "No Signal" over and over until he set it just right.

The local newscasters gushed about the presidential candidate who would be in town this week. They also covered a string of breaking and entering reports, a traffic jam on the interstate, and they closed out with sports, one last check on the weather, and a viral video of a kitten and a pug playing together. No mention of the clowns. No mention, so far as Phillip was concerned, of anything that actually mattered.

"What the heck?" he muttered to himself. "The public has a right to know!"

He flipped the TV off and stared at the blank screen a

while before he moved on. He shouldn't be surprised or disappointed that they'd ignored the message he'd left on the Channel 7 Hotline answering machine this morning, he knew. He should have seen this coming from miles away.

The police scanner barked cop jargon all through this. Most of it meant nothing to Phillip, but he knew that his mom knew all of the codes. Of course, he found the hobby a bit distasteful – ghoulish, even – finding entertainment in the emergencies and crimes happening around town.

He cleaned up after his meal, washing and drying the dishes and putting them away, erasing all evidence that anyone used the kitchen.

The daylight drained to a gray sky out the window while he worked. The days got so much shorter in October, and every year it caught him unaware. He wondered if that was something anyone ever got used to – the way everything around them never stopped changing.

"I'm going out for a walk," he said.

No matter how much trouble he was in, walking was the one thing he was always allowed to do – perhaps because his mother couldn't. He walked to his room and slid on a jacket, eyes catching the woods for just a second and remembering the clowns, but he pushed the thought away. It was just another thing that nobody wanted to believe, another awful truth he had to hold onto on his own.

"Be back before nine," she said, lifting her voice to be heard over the police chatter. "We can't have another tardy tomorrow morning, can we?"

# CHAPTER EIGHT

October 29th
6:27 PM

Instead of driving, she walked to Rick's, to clear her head and to prepare her break-up speech. She reminded herself again that Rick wasn't actually her boyfriend.

*Ahem.*

*Rick, I can't see you anymore.*

See him? Were they "seeing" each other?

*I don't think we should hang out anymore.*

Did that get the point across? Or should she be more firm?

*Listen, asshole. I'm done with you.*

Heh. That *did* sound more like Rick's style.

Her ribcage expanded and expelled a long sigh. Too bad she didn't have a friend she could talk to. Someone to tell her she was doing the right thing. Someone to back her up. Someone that would make sure she actually went through with it.

But she had no friends. There had been Molly, an older girl she met at a show. They'd hung out for a while. Molly was the one that had pierced her lip and nose. Molly's boyfriend was in one of the local grindcore bands, and a few months back, the band decided to move to LA. Molly had followed. She told Chloe she'd send a postcard when they got there, but she never did.

By eighth grade, almost all of the other girls in her grade had started to show signs of puberty. Faith was bemused to still be as flat-chested as ever, but Chloe was finally not the only girl with breasts. She wasn't totally immune to the staring and crude comments, still being more well-endowed than most of her peers and having been marked because she'd been the first. Boys still dropped pencils in front of her in an attempt to get her to bend over. Older men sometimes still had that wandering gaze. But it was less pronounced than before.

Or maybe she'd just started to get used to it.

That changed one day in gym class, when she noticed a group of boys in her class giggling. She turned around to find Greg Moffit standing behind her. He held a giant red wiffle ball bat to his crotch and was doing pelvic thrusts in Chloe's direction.

She told him to quit, but it was too late. Faith was also in their gym class, and she'd been trying all semester to get Greg's attention. Before Chloe could stop her, Faith ran crying to the girl's locker room.

Michelle Cousineau intercepted Chloe at the threshold of the locker room. She stood in the middle of the doorway, arms crossed in front of her like a bouncer at a club.

"Faith is very upset with you right now. You need to give her some space."

Chloe frowned. "But I didn't do anything."

"Chloe, we all saw what you did. You were practically drooling on Greg."

Chloe opened her mouth to respond then stopped herself.

OK, so she'd been smiling when she told Greg to quit. That was what she always did. She was afraid that if she showed how mad or embarrassed she was, it would just make things worse. She often tried to play it off like she was in on the joke. Like: *Haha, guys. Very funny. Now stop screwing around.*

Chloe tried to be patient with Faith. The whole thing would blow over eventually. But it didn't. Faith stopped talking to her and ignored Chloe's many attempts to apologize.

She was utterly convinced that Chloe was at fault. That she liked the attention. The thought made Chloe's lip curl in distaste. The irony, Chloe thought, was that Greg didn't even like her anyway. She was just a pair of boobs to him. An object. Not to mention the fact that him gyrating at her was hardly flirting in her book.

She wrote Faith note after note and text after text, begging her forgiveness. Eventually word got back to her that Faith was telling people that Chloe enjoyed how the boys teased and fawned over her. According to Faith, Chloe referred to herself as, "God's gift to men." Chloe tried to imagine those words coming out of her own mouth. It sounded more like something her mother would say. She suspected Michelle Cousineau had something to do with it. She'd always been envious of her closeness with Faith.

Eventually Chloe stopped apologizing. She figured that eventually things would go back to how they were. They had to. She and Faith were BFFs. That didn't just end.

Thinking back on it now, she remembered that Faith's

parents had been going through a divorce around that time. It made her former friend's actions make a little more sense but no less hurtful.

Chloe opened her locker one day to find that someone had slid something through the slats. It looked like a page from a magazine. She unfolded it to reveal a picture of her from an old yearbook, her face pasted onto the topless body of a Playboy playmate. She stared at the image, confused. Disgusted. Humiliated.

Laughter erupted behind her from a group that had no doubt been standing around to watch her reaction. She crumpled the glossy paper and threw it in the nearest trash bin. She didn't want to look back at them, but she couldn't resist. When she glanced back at the group, they were still laughing. All but Faith, who stood toward the back. Faith's eyes met Chloe's; a hard, cold stare, no trace of a smile.

When she got home from school that day, Chloe tore through her closet and dresser drawers, tearing anything that was too tight or too low cut from the hangers and tossing them into a heap at the center of her room. The wad of clothes got shoved into a garbage bag and put in the pile her parents kept in the basement for things they would eventually donate to the Salvation Army.

She started wearing the baggy t-shirts she normally wore to bed as pajamas. If she wore anything remotely formfitting, she made sure to wear a hoodie over top. It didn't really work. It wasn't like anyone was going to suddenly forget that she had big boobs just because she started wearing loose-fitting clothing. But she supposed the girls at least couldn't accuse her of asking for the attention anymore.

As she neared Rick's place, Chloe's pace grew slower and slower. When the house came into view, she stopped completely and jostled her lip ring from side to side with her tongue. Was this it? Was she actually going to do it?

*Remember how he always sneers when he mentions you going to school*, she told herself.

*Remember his stupid spiel about bum flaps being a lifestyle choice.*

*Remember that he's afraid of hitting the ground but not of falling.*

She nodded once and strode up the rotted wooden steps leading to the front door. The angle of the landing was off, and when she paused to open the door, she had a pang of vertigo.

The screen door – which was missing the screen, therefore maybe it was just a door – screeched as she pulled it wide. She didn't knock, because the door was never locked. That wasn't really how things worked at a squat. She just turned the knob and entered.

The aroma of the squat hit her like a slap in the face. It was a heady fragrance of piss, rotten food, stale cigarette smoke, and unwashed crusties.

Rick's room was up a rickety staircase, just as rotten and unstable as the one out front. Rick's door was the last one in the hallway, on the left. She swallowed before stepping into the dank chamber.

Her eyes did a quick scan, taking in the graffiti-covered walls and the bare, stained mattress in the corner. The mattress was empty, as was the rest of the room.

Damn it.

She gave a quick glance into each of the other rooms upstairs, but they were also vacant. Back down the stairs her booted feet stomped. There was no one in the kitchen or the dining room. The only person she could locate in the whole house was Malcolm.

He was passed out in a recliner in the living room. The same recliner she and Rick had been in when he sauntered in and puked all over the floor. Judging by the smell and the crusted stain that remained, no one had bothered to clean it up.

"Hey," she said.

Malcolm did not stir at her voice.

"Hey," she repeated, kicking the recliner this time. "You."

He still didn't move.

Chloe took a step closer, studying Malcolm. His greasy hair had fallen over his eyes, so she couldn't see his face very well. Christ, was he even breathing?

She bent over and touched his arm, to see if his skin was warm or cool. It was cool, kind of moist, like touching a frog.

She was breathing through her mouth because of the stench, and she couldn't help but feel like the day-old barf smell was permeating her nose and mouth and the pores of her skin. A sick feeling swelled in her gut.

"Malcolm?" She had meant to speak his name in an authoritative voice, but all she could muster was a hoarse whisper.

His name did nothing to rouse him.

Shit, he's actually dead, she thought. She retracted her hand from his clammy arm.

Suddenly his eyes snapped open, and he lurched upright in the chair. Chloe jumped back two paces.

"Huhwhat? Whatizzit?" His words were slurred, bleeding together in a jumbled mess.

"Christ! Jesus! Sorry!" Chloe said, taking another step away from him. "I thought you were fucking dead."

He slumped back into the chair, mouth slack, apparently unconcerned about his mortality. His mouth smacked opened and closed a few times, and she thought he might be tasting a few leftover morsels of vomit from the previous night.

She waited for him to say something, but he did not. She'd caught him mid-heroin stupor.

"More like heroin *stupid*," Rick always said.

Right. Rick.

Tapping her pinkie finger against her lip ring, Chloe soldiered on.

"So, uh, do you know if Rick's around?"

Malcolm shook his head.

"No, you don't know? Or no, he's not around?"

Malcolm was still shaking his head back and forth. Something about the sensation must have been pleasant in his high-as-a-kite state.

"Huh?"

"Do you know where Rick is?" She stressed each word, as if talking to an elderly person with bad hearing and a shaky grasp on reality. Which Malcolm basically was, for all intents and purposes.

"Oh. No, man. Haven't seen him today."

She puffed out her cheeks, stuffing her hands in her pockets. What could she do? If he wasn't here, he wasn't here.

She'd have to break up with Rick some other time.

"OK. Well, if you see him, will you tell him I stopped by?"

Malcolm was still rocking his head in a gesture that said, "No." But with his mouth, he said, "Sure. Right."

She turned to go, thinking that if Malcolm stayed awake enough to remember what she'd said for ten minutes, it would be a miracle. Just as she reached the hallway, he spoke again.

"You know, I don't think he ever came home last night."

She hung back.

"Really? Are you sure?"

Malcolm shrugged. "Didn't sleep in his room anyway, because I crashed out in there. He woulda kicked me offa his mattress when he came in. He always does. Rick doesn't like to cuddle."

Malcolm pulled his face into an exaggerated frown, like this hurt his feelings. Then he chuckled, and spit gurgled from between his lips. Before the screen door smacked shut behind Chloe, Malcolm was passed out again.

God damn junkies.

Chloe headed for the park, the only other place she'd ever gone with Rick other than venues and random, sketchy basements for shows.

On the way, she pondered whether or not Malcolm was full of shit. He was a junkie after all.

Where would Rick even go other than the squat? He had no real friends, no family that she knew of. Though he didn't really talk much about them other than to say they were, "a bunch of fucking deadbeat rednecks."

If Malcolm *wasn't* full of it... holy hell. Could Rick be

seeing someone else? Banging some chick on the side? Or maybe Chloe was the side chick. Though she was pretty sure to be a side chick you had to actually put out.

That sleazebag. That would be just like him. So very Rick.

God, why did she even care? Wasn't she here in the first place to tell him she never wanted to see him again?

As she rounded a curve in the path that led to the park, she saw something in the middle of the sidewalk ahead. The jumble of stuff didn't make sense to her eyes until she got closer and realized it was a bag.

No. Not just a bag.

Rick's bag.

She scooped the tattered, army green rucksack into her hands and looked around for a moment, thinking maybe he was nearby. She saw no one.

She rifled through the bag. A Circle Jerks 7-inch, even though he didn't have a turntable or the reliable source of electricity needed to power one. His Discman, which he favored over an mp3 player or phone because it ran on batteries instead of needing to be charged in an outlet or computer. An open bag of Cool Ranch Doritos which had leaked greasy crumbs all over the place. Candy wrappers. A toothbrush. Hairspray. A box of Trojan BareSkin condoms. Ew. For her? Or for the theoretical side chick?

Rick would never just leave his bag. It wasn't much, but his entire life was in that bag.

She imagined him going and getting more beer after she left, getting wasted in the park by himself, and then, stumbling back to the squat, getting jumped by a group of thugs. But if that was what happened, where was he?

She hurried on to the park, his bag slung over her shoulder.

The park, just like the squat and the surrounding streets, was empty.

Now what. Should she go back to the squat, try to badger more details out of Malcolm?

Screw that. He wasn't a dependable source of information.

Should she call the cops? God, Rick would just love that. If he showed up, unharmed, and found out she'd reported him missing to the police, he'd be furious. Or maybe he'd laugh and call her a pussy.

If she did call the cops, she'd probably have to mention the squat, and then all those guys would be screwed. They'd hate her guts. She'd be branded a narc for eternity. No more shows. She'd get her ass kicked if she showed her face after getting a bunch of guys booted from their squat.

Scratch the cops, then.

Her parents? A short, bitter laugh came out of her then, and she thought of how that conversation would go.

"So, mom, the twenty-year-old vagrant I'm dating is missing. His heroin addict squat-mate said he never came home last night, and I found his bag dumped on the trail a couple blocks from his house. His name? Oh, everybody just calls him Rick Dagger, because he supposedly stabbed someone once."

Ha.

Ha.

No.

Not happening.

It wasn't until she passed the alley where she'd seen the

clown that it occurred to her that Rick's disappearance and the clown may somehow be connected.

The police were out. She had no friends. Her not-boyfriend was mysteriously missing. And her parents treated her like a pariah almost as much as peers did.

But there was still someone she could turn to.

"Fuck me," she said under her breath.

Turdholder.

# CHAPTER NINE

October 29th
6:41 PM

Moffit kneeled in the tall grass to relieve the ache in his legs from squatting for so long. The moisture from his breath clung to the inside of the mask, clammy cheeks slicked and sliding up against the rubber. It felt awful.

"How do we… " Danny said. "What do we do if, like, he never comes out?"

"What's it been? Ten minutes? Just wait. He'll come out."

"How do you know?"

"How do I know? Look, you got somewhere more important to be?"

Danny didn't answer for a second.

"Well, no."

"Then zip it."

The words sounded strange coming out of Moffit's mouth, and not just because they were muffled by the latex stretched across his lips. They were his father's words. Whenever he was annoyed, and he just wanted to watch football, which was most of the time, that was what he said. "Zip it." Jesus. No one Greg's age said zip it.

His face flushed under the mask. The warmth radiated out from his cheeks, a slow swelling of the temperature, and he was happy to have the clown face sheathed over his own to

70

conceal the redness that he was certain accompanied the heat.

The glass apartment door swung open then, and Moffit held his breath for that beat as the figure took shape in the doorframe. An old lady with blue reusable grocery bags dangling from her hands. Damn.

Moffit was sure that Danny was about to make some smartass remark, and he clenched his teeth to brace himself for the annoyance, but the comment never came. Well… good. Maybe he was done complaining for a while. That'd be nice.

The old lady's taillights spilled a red glow over the parking lot, and then she was gone.

"Did you…" Danny said, turning to stare into the dark behind them. "I think I heard something. In the woods."

"Probably just the car pulling out. The tires rolled over bits of gravel, and it echoed funny."

"No, bro. There's someone out here."

Moffit's spine stiffened, the rigidity pulling him all the way upright. He listened. His breath was loud against the latex, so he held it.

Nothing. No sounds but the occasional car whooshing by every so often.

"I don't hear shit," he said, letting the muscles in his back slacken a touch.

"Yeah," the red-haired boy said. "Yeah, maybe it was nothing."

Danny didn't quite believe it was nothing, but in truth, he'd been scared since before they even set foot in the woods, and it was now getting hard to distinguish paranoia from reality. Maybe it *was* nothing. He hoped so.

Here we go again, Danny figured. He always got dragged along on Moffit's adventures. Too scared to say no. Too scared to admit he was frightened of or disgusted by most of the things they did. So here he was, cowering out in the woods, waiting around to spook some kid he barely knew, his bladder aching with that stabbing, feverish pain of being too full. But he was too scared to wander off and take a leak by himself, of course.

He'd always been scared of new people, new things. Scared of asserting himself. In kindergarten, he'd been too scared to tell the teacher he had to go to the bathroom, slinking off to the corner and pissing himself instead.

Maybe that was how he wound up aligning himself with a bully like Moffit. Cruel or not, Moffit was strong. Fearless. A leader for a lemming to follow. A lemming like me, he thought.

The wait stretched out a while, though, and they remained silent. Something like a calm came over Danny. A trance almost, he thought. Like he'd been hypnotized into forgetting his fear.

"Oh shit. There he is," Moffit said.

"Huh?"

"Second floor. Third window from the right."

The scrawny figure filling the window frame was Turdholder, all right, and it looked like he was sliding on a jacket.

"Fuck yeah," Moffit said. "I knew he'd come out sooner or later. We're about to do this."

Moffit rocked forward so that he was standing up on his knees, his posture taut with anticipation.

"Keep that phone ready."

The surge of adrenaline that came with the excitement pushed Danny over the edge. The stab in his bladder intensified from a needle prick to the thrust of a broad sword. Time to go. Immediately.

"So hey, I have to piss real quick."

"What? Christ. Hurry up."

He clambered up onto his feet, his legs numb and prickling from so much time crouching. A few crashing footsteps concealed him in the taller brush, and he fumbled at his zipper.

The urine skimmed the blades of grass and slapped at the ground. The relief poured into his skull, a wave of euphoria washing over his brain. There was no pleasure in life quite like letting go like this.

After the last few drops were shaken free, he zipped up and turned to head back. He prepped the phone once more, fully ready now to scare the bejesus out of Turdholder and be done with this. He started filming, a little smile curling his lip now that this was almost over.

A thought interrupted the relief, however, shattering the post-urinal bliss. Moffit had been quiet this whole time. Eerily quiet.

He eased back the five paces to where they'd been, the fear returning all at once, his heart hammering at the walls of his chest. God, just let it be paranoia again.

He stepped out of the shadows to the cleared out spot their feet had trampled in the grass. He saw Moffit hunched there, arms hugged around his middle and wiggling, and he was relieved once more to find his friend alive and moving.

But then he heard the moist sounds – little pats and slaps, not unlike the noise of a dog licking the hairless patch of flesh in its armpit.

The phone light caught the crouched boy's torso and that which glistened below his wriggling arms. His middle was wet. Red. Opened up.

Danny gasped, the reality of what he was looking at occurring to him bit by bit.

Greg Moffit was desperately trying to shove his intestines back into his abdomen and having little success. He pawed at the guts with cupped hands, pushing the strands around as much as anything, like a child trying to scoop up spaghetti with a spoon.

"Shit," Moffit said almost inaudibly. Based on the deadpan delivery, Danny knew he must be in shock, must not know or understand exactly what was happening here.

"Oh, Jesus, Greg," he hissed, eyes glued to the tubes slithering out of his friend's belly. "Are you OK?"

"Obviously fucking not," Moffit said.

His head bobbed up so he could glare at Danny.

Blood throbbed out of his belly in sheets, the muscles contracting in wild bursts. He coughed, the hack choking itself into a gurgle as the blood caught in his throat, and then he coughed again, the thick red spluttering out to drain down his chin.

The shock of this spectacle threw Danny so thoroughly that he hadn't quite considered how it had happened to Moffit. He backpedaled without thought, like he could just drift away from this scene, and it wouldn't be real anymore.

A twig snapped behind him, and he jumped straight up.

He would have pissed himself if he hadn't just gone. He whirled to find exactly what he'd feared he would.

The clowns stood before him, six of them, weapons hanging limp at their sides, their legs just more than shoulder width apart. All eyes locked on his.

His throat closed up, clenching like some strange sphincter at the back of his mouth. He could muster no great scream, not even so much as an exaggerated gasping inhale. He blinked. Otherwise, he was motionless.

Moffit watched the clowns close on his friend, leaving his wound to witness the fresh horror before him. He was cold, so cold, the warmth draining out of him along with his blood. He lived long enough to see the axe split Danny's head and to see the clowns surround the fallen body to feast.

He lay back, head settling in the tall grass, and he looked up into the heavens, finding that gray clouds swathed everything up there. And that was all. No light flared in the sky above. No calm or peace came over him as his life slipped away. He was very cold and very alone.

# CHAPTER TEN

October 30th
7:06 AM

The cold stung in Phillip's nose and in the tips of his fingers. This was the chilliest morning yet, and it was the first time this school year that waiting for the bus had bordered on unbearable. It was hard to believe that it would only get colder and harsher from here as winter came around.

Frost coated the ground, a sparkling layer atop the grass that twinkled in the early morning light. His eyes couldn't help themselves. They kept tracing the frosted shimmer to its edge, glancing at the place where the grass ended and the woods began. The place where the clowns had been. The foliage there looked a little disturbed, he thought, the tall grass all mashed down in one area, but it was hard to be sure from this distance. Maybe he was just being paranoid.

The bus arrived, the door swinging open with a hiss, and he climbed the steps into the warmth, the cold and the clowns once more vacating his thoughts. The atmosphere on the bus was subdued this morning. Quiet. Sleepy. He closed his eyes upon taking his seat, the heat enveloping him, and he drifted into a half-sleep state.

His mind went blank, focusing only on the sensation swelling back into his hands and nose, on the heat settling over him like blanket. It was a pleasant feeling. A peaceful one.

After what seemed like no more than a minute, the engine's vibration changed as the bus idled in front of the school, waking him. He filed back into the cold along with the others, all of the pressures of the impending day seeping back into his consciousness.

He'd only taken two steps onto the concrete when he heard the voice call out from behind him.

"Phillip."

He stopped, his shoulders scrunching up along the sides of his neck involuntarily, a gesture that looked like someone who'd just gotten splashed with frigid water. He turned.

A girl sat in a Chrysler Le Baron there, glaring out the open window, eyebrows raised in anticipation of his response. He recognized her by sheer quantity of eyeliner as much as anything. It was Chloe Trepper. Though he knew who she was, he didn't know her personally apart from all of the crazy rumors he'd heard. She was a witch, some said. Others said she boiled and ate her pet rat. Still others claimed that she'd masturbated with a frozen hot dog at Shelly Kwiatkoski's party. He didn't quite buy these things, but even so, he couldn't think of any reason in the universe that she would talk to him voluntarily.

He looked around, trying to spot someone else she might be talking to, but everyone else had hustled in to get out of the cold. He pointed a finger at his chest, poking it into his coat three times, the international hand signal for, "You talking to me?"

"Yeah, you," she said. "Get in."

She tilted her head toward the passenger seat as she said it.

Again, he looked around. This couldn't be real.

"But school is about to start?"

"I know about the clown," she said.

His posture went rigid, snapping upright as though he'd just suffered a slight electrical shock. He thought for a moment.

"Well… I just got a tardy in art yesterday, so I'm kind of on thin ice."

The girl rolled her eyes.

"This is more important than school. Now get in the damn car, Turdholder."

"Look, I can't say it any plainer. I'm not getting another tardy. I just did hard time in detention yesterday, and I'm in no hurry to go back."

Phillip turned and headed into the building before she could argue the matter further.

"Phillip!"

Her cry was swallowed by the glass door swinging closed so that the second syllable was almost inaudible. Strange girls pressuring him to skip school? This was more unbelievable than the armed clowns in the woods.

"Has the whole world gone insane?" he muttered to himself.

To Phillip's surprise, art class came and went without event. Moffit was absent along with his red-haired lackey. That made things easier. He kept his head down as usual, his construction paper mosaic of a dog coming together nicely. He enjoyed the quiet.

The first half of the day slipped by, and he forgot all about the events in front of the school that morning, the strange girl in the Le Baron beckoning.

He had Beef Stroganoff for lunch. Not his favorite, but it wasn't crusty around the edges, at least. He'd eaten worse things in the cafeteria.

He doodled in the margin of his notebook paper during social studies, a twisted braid of vines that worked its way toward the top of the page as the teacher droned on. It was one of the only things he drew. He didn't know why.

Mr. Neiderhauser had a knack for putting people to sleep, his monotone almost more soothing than it was boring, Phillip thought. Maybe the class falling just after lunch somehow assisted in inducing people to slumber. Phillip wasn't sure, but he drew to stay awake.

Neiderhauser's monk chant cut out for a beat, but Phillip didn't bother looking up. He wove more vines around each other.

"Phillip," Niederhauser said. "You're, uh, needed in the office."

His pen stopped, and he looked up to the front of the room. In a way, he was surprised to see who had come to fetch him, and yet it seemed somehow inevitable at the same time.

It was her. The hot dog witch herself. Chloe. One hand on her hip, she smirked at him, looking quite pleased with her charade.

"Should I bring my stuff?" he said, not knowing why he asked.

"Better bring it," she said, smirk erased and replaced with mock gravity. "It sounded serious."

He fumbled with his books, certain his cheeks had those pink blotches they got when something embarrassed him.

He followed her into the hallway. The skim and clatter of their feet moving over the floors resonated around them like a soft backbeat to this awkward scene. Something about the sound made the hall itself seem cavernous, Phillip thought. The school building felt different than usual. They were two tiny beings alone in a strange place.

"This is pretty fudged up," he said, keeping his voice hushed now that they moved in the quiet of the hall. "Pulling me out of social studies like that. Are you even an office aide?"

"Of course not."

"Nice. Just perfect. I guess I'll just flunk social studies on top of geometry. No big whoop."

"It couldn't be helped, I'm afraid. We have matters to attend to. Clown matters."

"And these matters couldn't wait until after school?"

The place between her eyebrows creased a moment.

"That's actually a good point. I hadn't thought about it that way. We probably could have waited."

Phillip threw his hands up.

"Un-fudgin-believable."

She looked around, barely seeming tethered to their conversation.

"Too late now. Which reminds me, if you see any hall monitors, you should probably hide."

"Just me?"

"Huh? No, me too. Both of us should hide."

"OK. It's just that the way you said it, it kind of sounded

**80**

like you meant that just I would need to-"

Phillip's explanation was cut off by Chloe grabbing him, both hands latching around his left wrist and tugging full force. He followed her involuntarily, catching himself from falling over with cloppy steps, an uneven stagger that led him out of the hallway and into the...

No.

No, it couldn't be.

She'd pulled him into the girl's restroom. It smelled vaguely of baby powder, unlike the boy's restroom which had more of a dehydrated urine and diarrhea odor.

"This is..."

"Look, I know it's utterly fudged, but we need to hide out here for a minute," Chloe said, and he was pretty sure she was mocking him with the fudge thing. She pointed a thumb at the hallway. "Hall monitor creeping out there. I don't think he saw us, but..."

Phillip couldn't stop scanning for some place to hide. Could he crouch behind the garbage can, scooting it in such a way so as to pen himself into the corner? Should he huddle in one of the stalls, climbing up onto the seat so his shoes wouldn't be visible if the hall monitor burst through the door and stalked from toilet to toilet?

What if someone came in? Say some girl needed to waltz in here and take a big ol' donkey crap before gym class?

He took a step back at the thought, edging away from the stalls, his elbow catching on a metal box attached to the wall. He glanced at it, doing a double-take.

Tampon machine.

Phillip's vision went swimmy along the edges. Sweat

**81**

beaded on his forehead, thick droplets of perspiration sogging into his brow. Was this a panic attack? He thought this might be a panic attack.

"You OK?" Chloe said, after looking at him for a long time.

"What? Yeah, I'm fine."

"He should be gone by now. Let's move."

They pushed through the doorway and fled the building, Phillip holding his breath until he was safely sealed inside the car.

# CHAPTER ELEVEN

October 30th
1:39 PM

Vinyl squeaked as Chloe scooted over the cushioned booth. The door to the kitchen swung open and for a moment, the sizzling of the flat top and the gurgle of the fryer grease could be heard. The delightful smell of French fries and bacon and coffee wafted over to their table, and Chloe's mouth watered. A waitress walked by with a double decker club sandwich and a giant pile of onion rings. Chloe's stomach grumbled. Man, she was starving.

She yawned. Tired, too. She hadn't slept well again. She had paced around her room until 3 AM, too jacked up on adrenaline to sleep.

She glanced over at Phillip. He held the laminated menu up so it obscured most of his face, and his eyes shifted from side to side.

Chloe leaned back in the booth.

"You alright over there, Turdholder?"

His eyes stopped roaming and studied her.

"It's called keeping a low profile," he said. "I would assume that a delinquent such as yourself would be well versed in the art of being inconspicuous."

Delinquent, eh? He gave her a snotty look and then went back to perusing his menu. Chloe smirked to herself.

It was funny. Chloe had never been in trouble with the law, and she even got decent grades. But Phillip was not the only one that took one look at her and thought, "screw up." Most people, she'd found, were extremely superficial that way.

It hardly bothered her anymore. She'd had three years to get used to it.

She picked up a spoon and tapped it against her lip ring. *Click click click.*

The old Chloe, the one that had long blond hair and played soccer and volleyball, thought she knew what people were really like. But the old Chloe didn't know shit.

That all changed in eighth grade.

Twas the night before Picture Day. Chloe's mother was in her room, helping her decide how to do her hair for her yearbook photo. Hanging on the outside of her closet was the outfit they'd chosen at the beginning of the year. A white lace blouse layered over a shell pink tank top, and though the neckline was high enough to mostly conceal her ample cleavage, Chloe still hated it for two reasons. One, it was much too form-fitting compared to all the baggy shirts she'd started wearing. Two, the lace was too feminine. Lace was for panties and bras and teddies. The last thing she wanted to be associated with.

"I changed my mind about what I'm going to wear," Chloe said. "I think I'm just going to wear my striped polo shirt instead."

"Uh," her mom said, tugging a brush through Chloe's hair. "I don't think so, missy."

"Why not?"

A hair got caught in the brush and Chloe winced.

"Because, we picked that out especially for picture day. We both agreed."

"But I don't want to wear it anymore."

Her mom stopped coifing and put a fist on her hip, studying her daughter. "Why are you being difficult?"

Chloe was too embarrassed to tell her about Faith and Greg Moffit and really just about everyone else at school. About how the boys stared and the girls whispered. About the teachers that constantly battled with their inner horndog, eyes bouncing from Chloe's breasts to her face like they were reading the words to a sing-along song on TV.

Or maybe it was how her mom phrased it. That yet again, this was something Chloe was doing. She didn't ask what was wrong, or just "Why not?"

*Why are* you *being difficult?*

Chloe picked at the stitching on her quilted bedspread.

"It doesn't fit me anymore," she said. "I guess I gained weight."

Chloe thought this might elicit some sympathy. Her mom was always on some kind of diet and obsessed over whether or not she was currently able to fit in her "skinny clothes."

She got no such reaction. Instead, her mother insisted that Chloe try the outfit on.

Begrudgingly, Chloe changed into the white and pink ensemble.

"I don't know what you're talking about," her mom said. "It fits you perfectly. Like a glove."

That's the problem, Chloe thought.

"Your real problem is that you need to stand up straight,

like this," her mother said, sticking out her own chest. "Roll your shoulders back, and stop hunching like an old crone."

Right, mom, Chloe thought. Stick 'em out. Loud and proud.

She sighed. "Can I please wear something else?"

"Chloe Marie Trepper, I paid good money for those clothes, and it's way past the 30 day return policy. You are wearing that outfit, missy."

Maybe seeing how dejected Chloe looked or possibly just trying to smooth it over, her mother added, "But how about this, honey? You can pick how you want to wear your hair."

The next morning, her mother got up early with her, supposedly to help Chloe with her hair. Chloe had a sneaking suspicion it was really to make sure she was indeed wearing the lace blouse they'd picked out.

As her mother yanked at her hair, subjecting her to the blow dryer and the curling iron, Chloe's eyes fell on her father's electric razor sitting on the edge of the counter.

Turdholder's voice broke in, parting the cloud of memory that had enveloped Chloe for the last several minutes.

"What are we doing here anyway? Are we meeting up with some... er... contacts?"

Something that was part laugh and part cough crackled in Chloe's throat.

"Contacts?"

"Other people sympathetic to the cause?"

"And what cause would that be? The P.A.C.C.? People Against Creepy Clowns?"

Phillip's brow wrinkled, and he dipped his head forward, looking deadly serious.

"Is that a thing?"

Chloe laughed in earnest then.

"Phillip. Dude. There are no contacts. It's just me and you. And we are here," she lifted a finger and drew a circle in the air, "because I didn't eat breakfast or lunch, and now I'm fucking starving."

The waitress appeared to take their order. Phillip stayed hidden behind his menu as he requested the chicken finger platter and seemed reluctant to part with the laminated sheet when the waitress put out a hand to collect it.

Chloe ordered cheese fries, mozzarella sticks, and a Coke, and Phillip muttered something under his breath about soft drinks being like battery acid on the teeth.

He must have been feeling naked without his menu to hide behind, and Chloe watched him lift a napkin to keep the lower half of his face concealed.

Chloe leaned forward conspiratorially.

"Hey, I have a disguise kit in the car, you know. Fake mustaches and whatnot."

He shifted the napkin away from his mouth. "Seriously? Why didn't you say so?"

Chloe just grinned, and she watched his face change as it dawned on him that she was messing with him.

"You know, that's very funny. But I don't think you'll be laughing too hard if we get spotted. Truancy is a serious offense."

Ah. So he was still paranoid about ditching school. She thought it might be that, but she also hadn't discounted the idea that he didn't want to be seen socializing with Chloe the Freak.

Chloe sat through her first two classes on eighth grade picture day, wearing a baggie University of Michigan hoodie over the lace top her mother had insisted upon. During her third hour English class, the students were called down to the gymnasium, one by one, to have their pictures taken.

"Chloe," Mrs. Posnansky announced from the front of the room. "You're up."

On the way to the gym, Chloe made a detour to her locker and then to the bathroom. Under the buzzing florescent lights, she stared at her reflection in the mirror and wondered if she actually had the guts to do it. Her teeth ground together, and she plugged the cord into the outlet on the wall. Her thumb found the switch, flicked it, and the electric razor hummed to life.

When Chloe reached the gym, there was a line of five students from other classes waiting ahead of her. They jostled each other and whispered upon seeing her. She waited for one of them to make some kind of remark as she took her place in line. But a curious thing happened instead. They all fell silent.

The photographer, a good-looking guy she guessed to be in his thirties, did stare at her. But not at her chest for once. He couldn't take his eyes off her freshly shaved head.

And it was different still. He did it only when he thought she wasn't looking, though she caught him gaping out of the corner of her eye. To his credit, he said nothing about it, joking with her and doing his best to get her to smile when her photograph was taken. She did not smile for the picture, though. When she was through, he gave her a thumbs up and said, "Stay strong!"

# The Clowns

She understood then. He thought she had cancer.

Hushed whispers filled the room when she returned to class. Enough that Mrs. Posnansky looked up from her desk. Her eyes followed Chloe all the way to her seat.

Yes, there was whispering. Yes, there was staring. But honestly, she was surprised there wasn't more of a reaction. She'd expected someone to say something. An open confrontation. Before, if she'd even so much as gotten up to use the pencil sharpener and caught one of the boys staring, they'd call her Jugs or pantomime something sexual in nature.

But this was different. Everyone was so careful not to let her see them staring.

Mrs. Posnansky sent the next person in line down to the gym, a girl named Phoebe Trethaway. Before Phoebe left, Mrs. Posnansky whispered something to her. A few minutes later, there was a light knock at the door.

Chloe felt the teacher glance at her on her way to answer the door. There were more hushed voices, and then she saw Mr. Philbrooks, the principal, poke his head into the room. His eyes roved over the sea of students before landing on Chloe. He looked alarmed, like a bird startled by a creeping house cat. He withdrew his head immediately. The murmuring outside the door resumed, and then she heard Mr. Philbrooks clear his throat.

"Ahh, Ms. Trepper..." he trailed off. "Could you come out here?"

Christ, was she in trouble? Was it against the rules to shave your head at school or something?

She gathered her books, unsure if this was a permanent removal from class or not, and went out into the hallway.

**89**

Usually, such a summons would cause some "oohs" from the other students. Maybe a taunting, "Someone's in trouble!" They were notably silent that day.

She exited the classroom and Mr. Philbrooks closed the door behind her. He licked his lips, still staring, apparently unsure how to proceed

"Chloe," he said, crossing his arms. "Could you tell us what happened? Is there... something going on that we should know about?"

"Like what?" Chloe asked. Did he think she was being abused or something? She wasn't sure what he was getting at.

"Are you," he glanced at Mrs. Posnansky, "sick?"

It was a beat before it dawned on Chloe exactly what he meant. Right. The cancer thing again. She blinked.

"Sure," she said, nodding. "I'm sick. Sick and tired of all the bullshit."

The look on their faces? God, it was priceless.

Mr. Philbrooks took her by the arm and yanked her down to his office.

Their food arrived and Chloe practically dove headfirst into the cheese fries. Phillip huffed a breath out of his nose, and she stopped chewing just long enough to say, "What?"

With both his hands placed face down on the table, he gazed at her levelly.

"We aren't going to say Grace?"

"Knock yourself out," she said, dunking a mozzarella stick into a cup of blood red marinara.

Phillip's face got a little red, but then he composed himself. Bowing his head, he closed his eyes, took a deep breath, and muttered a few prayers to himself. Chloe resisted the urge to take another bite of food until he was finished.

"Amen," he said, then took up his knife and fork. Chloe wouldn't have thought it was possible to eat fried chicken fingers in a prissy manner, but somehow Turdholder found a way.

His eyes flicked up at her a few times while he ate. The way he avoided eye contact reminded her of how they said not to look a mean dog in the eyes. At least he'd stopped hiding behind his napkin.

A strand of melty cheese oozed out of one of the deep-fried sticks, and she wrapped it around her finger.

For a while they didn't talk. They just ate.

Phillip dabbed daintily at the corners of his mouth and then folded his napkin, placing it on the table.

"Well?" he asked.

Chloe picked up a crumb of bacon leftover from her cheese fries and popped it in her mouth.

"What?"

"You practically dragged me here as your hostage." Chloe rolled her eyes, but he continued. "I assume there was a reason for it."

"You saw a clown. I saw a clown. Don't you think we should compare notes?"

"First of all, I saw *clowns*. As in plural. As in five of them."

She waited for him to go on, but he did not.

"What's the 'second of all?'"

"Nothing! I saw five clowns. That's it."

She slid her phone out of her pocket and set it on the table. A greasy smear was left behind when she swiped the screen. Before proceeding, she licked her finger clean.

A map appeared.

"Show me where you saw them."

Flicking his finger over the map, Phillip scrolled until he found what he was looking for. "Here."

Chloe leaned closer to take a look.

"That's only a few blocks from where I found Rick's bag."

"Who's Rick?"

"My... friend," she said. She'd almost made the mistake of adding *boy* in front of *friend*. "He never made it home last night, and then I found his bag just abandoned a couple blocks from his house. I figured the clown thing has to be connected."

She jabbed at the screen with a black fingernail.

"Rick's bag was here. I saw one somewhere over in this area. You saw them here. They aren't very far apart." The map zoomed out. "And look. There are all those woods right there. Maybe they've got some kind of... I don't know... clown lair hidden in there."

She waited for Phillip to say how ridiculous that sounded. Clown lair? Had those words actually come out of her mouth?

Instead, he nodded. "Yeah. OK. That would make sense."

When he didn't say more, she stated what she felt was the obvious.

"We should go check it out."

Phillip recoiled as if she'd physically pushed him.

"Absolutely not. This is a police matter, obviously."

With one eyebrow raised, Chloe tilted her head and stared him down, not speaking.

"I assume you've filed a police report about your missing

friend. It *is* your civic duty."

Vinyl creaked as she pressed her back into the cushion.

"Right, and that worked out so well for you. You know everyone thinks you made it up."

Phillip closed his eyes and waggled his head back and forth. "That's a simple misunderstanding."

"A misunderstanding that could be cleared up if we go out there and find proof of this evil clown activity."

His head kept on shaking, lips pressed together in a line.

Chloe leaned in and lowered her voice, trying to sound grave. "Is it not sometimes a citizen's duty to take matters into their own hands, if that's what it takes to keep the public safe?"

Phillip's head stilled, and he squinted at her.

"I feel like you're twisting my words," he said, rubbing a knuckle along his jaw. "But I suppose if we found some hard evidence that we could take to the police, something that would convince them to take us seriously... that would be judicious."

Chloe slapped her hand on the table top.

"See? That's what I'm saying. Super judicious."

# CHAPTER TWELVE

October 30th
3:26 PM

The engine idled and cut out as Chloe parked the car next to the playground where she'd last seen Rick.

The day felt different now. When they were talking about it in the restaurant, it had seemed more like an adventure. But now that they were out here, out where it felt a little desolate despite being in the city, there was something more ominous about the whole thing.

She climbed out and closed her door more gently than usual, not wanting to slam it for some reason. There was a dull *thunk* as she locked the doors and pocketed the keys.

The two swings in the playground moved freely in the breeze, and Chloe couldn't stop herself from imagining a pair of ghost friends sitting in them. Rick's ghost? Nope. Stop thinking about creepy stuff. Besides, she thought, Rick's ghost wouldn't be playing on a damn playground. He'd be trying to figure out a way to get his non-corporeal hands on cheap beer and underage booty.

The wind kicked up, rustling through the dry leaves. A metal road sign shuddered in the gust, emitting an eerie whine that sent a cold shiver up her spine.

Chloe felt jittery. Too many Coke refills at the diner. She pulled her hoodie tight around her body and zipped it all the way up to her neck.

Midway between the playground and the squat, she stopped and pointed at the ground.

"This is where I found the bag."

Phillip nodded, then began circling the area, eyes on the ground. When he reached the chain-link fence that bordered the sidewalk, he dropped to his knees and began sifting through the pile of dead leaves collected there.

Chloe jammed her fists in her hoodie pocket.

"What are you doing?"

He paused only briefly to give her a patronizing look before he returned to sweeping the leaves away.

"Uh, looking for proof. Isn't that the whole point of us being out here?"

The tip of Chloe's tongue jabbed at her lip ring and wiggled it to and fro.

"And what exactly do you think you're gonna find down there? Clown droppings?"

Phillip scoffed.

"It's called trace evidence. Have you ever even seen an episode of CSI?" Leaves swished under his hands as he pawed at them. The way he used both hands to clear them away reminded Chloe of someone swimming the breast stroke. Phillip continued. "You're the one that dragged me out here on this flippin' goosechase."

Before she could come up with a witty retort, Phillip gasped and froze.

"Oh geez. Oh my good gravy."

From her position, Phillip and the heap of leaves he'd scooped out of the way obscured her view of whatever he'd found.

"What is it?" She took a step closer and saw the red stains on the concrete. "Holy shit. Is that blood?"

Phillip scurried away from the spot, but Chloe moved in on it, crouching to get a better look at the splatters.

She let out a long sigh, realizing only then that she'd been holding her breath.

"Relax. It's just red spray paint."

"How can you tell?"

"Because blood would have dried and turned brown by now. And look," she pointed to a patch of graffiti on the wall of a nearby building. The tag was the same shade of red as the paint on the sidewalk.

"Phew," Phillip said. He attempted to laugh, but it sounded forced. "Now what?"

Chloe pointed to where the path led further into the wooded area. And though golden leaves could be seen drifting to the ground like confetti, she couldn't help but feel a sense of foreboding.

Their feet crunched over the path. The warm glow from the afternoon light filtering through the yellow and red canopy above them gave the forest an enchanted aura. Chloe started to feel silly at how spooked she'd gotten before. She got out a cigarette and lit it. A piece of stray tobacco stuck to her lip, and she brushed it off with a finger.

"So it's true, then?" Phillip said, as if continuing some prior conversation. "You're a witch?"

She snorted.

"People are so judgmental. You eat the heart of the frog

you were dissecting for biology class *one time,* and everyone acts like you've gone over to the dark side."

He stopped walking and just stared at her.

"Phillip, I'm kidding! Jesus."

She tore a sassafras leaf from a branch and shredded it into tiny bits.

"Is this about me not saying Grace before? Just because I don't swallow all the bullshit like everyone else doesn't mean I'm a witch. Or a satanist. Or whatever else they call me."

Chloe shook her head, taking a long drag on the cigarette. She couldn't believe that even Phillip Turdholder bought into that crap.

Her mother was – not shockingly – furious over the head-shaving incident.

"What were you thinking? And what's going on down at that school of yours that kids can just shave their heads willy-nilly? Is anyone even watching what you're doing or is it a free-for-all?"

Chloe smirked. Willy-nilly. Such a mom phrase. The rant continued.

"Do you have any idea how long that's going to take to grow out? You look like a cancer patient! What am I going to tell people? This is so embarrassing."

Chloe's anger – at first just a mild simmer – raged into a full boil. Of course her mother would make this about herself and about how Chloe was *humiliating* her. So typical.

"Why? Why would you do something like this?"

Chloe very calmly answered, "I wore your fucking outfit, didn't I? You said I got to pick how I wore my hair."

Her mother's nostrils flared, and she jabbed a finger toward the stairs. "Your room. Now. You are grounded, missy. You hear me? Grounded!"

It was the first of many ineffective groundings. When Chloe came home with the most recent addition to her piercing collection – her lip – her mother hadn't even bothered.

"Put as many holes in your head as you want. What do I care?"

Chloe immediately imagined herself with a bullet hole in her forehead. Had her mother meant it to sound like that? Or was she only talking about more piercings?

In any case, it wouldn't have mattered if she *had* grounded Chloe. For one, she barely had anything to be grounded from. For two, the last three times she'd been grounded, it hadn't stopped her from sneaking out her window to go to shows or Rick's or sometimes to just walk around town at night.

At school, she heard many explanations for her shaved head. Her favorite was the one where she'd cut off her hair as a sacrifice to the devil. No one bothered to actually ask her the real reason. She supposed she wasn't totally sure herself back then. It had been a mostly impulsive act. When she took the razor that day, she hadn't even been sure she had the balls to do it. It was mostly a fantasy until the moment the vibrating shears took away a section of her golden hair. And then she knew she had to go all the way.

It was strange, really. She felt a power in her otherness now. Before, when it had been about her body, she'd despised it. But now, when it was more about her being a head-shaving weirdo, there was something comforting in the way people stared. She was in control. She had chosen this.

Of course there were moments of despair. She was still lonely and missed having friends. Having someone to sit with at lunch. Someone to text when the teacher wasn't looking. But she wasn't surprised at the superficiality of her peers.

But no one dared to look at her chest or try to grab her now. Her male teachers would barely look her in the eyes. It was a while before she realized that they were afraid of her.

When Chloe's hair grew out a bit, she dyed it black with a package of hair dye she bought from Walgreens. This further enraged her mother, who rushed her to a salon and told them to do whatever it took to get it back to Chloe's natural hair color. They over-bleached it, leaving Chloe with platinum locks.

"Better than that ghastly black. What are you, a Satan worshiper now?" her mother said on the drive home from the salon. "You shave your head, quit soccer and volleyball, and now this? What's gotten into you?"

Better, indeed, Chloe thought. She ordered more dye off the internet the next day, using the new platinum as a blank slate for a bright blood red. Her mother was practically hysterical.

"I am done. Done! Do you hear me? I have half a mind to send you to one of those boot camps so someone else can straighten you out."

Back to the salon they went, where the stylist informed her mother that any further bleaching would likely cause Chloe's hair to break off or fall out. Her mother raged at them for a while before giving up.

A rumor went around that she had boiled and skinned her

pet rat and used its blood to dye her hair red. She shook her head, almost laughing to herself. Seriously? She didn't even have a pet rat. Where the hell did they come up with this stuff?

As they got deeper into the woods, the sounds of the city vanished. Chloe could no longer hear traffic in the distance. It smelled good, too. Like rain and leaves and maybe even a little bit of dirt, but in a pleasant way. She thought about lighting another cigarette but decided against it. She wanted to enjoy the fresh fall air for a little while longer.

Her fingers discovered something in her hoodie pocket then. It was hard and round. Pinching it between her fingers, she pulled it free. She didn't immediately recognize the small, yellow sphere, but then she realized it was a Lemonhead that must have escaped the box yesterday. Sweet, she thought. Pocket candy.

She popped it into her mouth.

"So what else have you heard?"

Phillip swung his head around to face her. "Pardon?"

"About me. What other juicy gossip?" She held the candy between her gums and her cheek while she spoke.

"I hadn't heard the frog thing before, actually."

"Yeah, I made that one up myself."

"What? Why?"

"I don't know. Just seemed like something people would say about me. Or believe about me."

They walked on, leaves crunching underfoot.

"I remember hearing something about you putting a hex on your math teacher for giving you a bad grade."

"Right! I forgot about that one." Chloe clapped her hands together. "Did you hear the one where I had a voodoo doll of the principal that I was using to get free hall passes?"

"I heard that it was a voodoo doll of the football coach you were using to make them lose their games."

"Nice!" She chuckled. "I hadn't heard that variation. As if they need my help losing games. They suck enough on their own."

"Oh, and then there was the thing with the hot do-"

Phillip's voice cut off, and Chloe watched bright pink splotches form on his cheeks.

"The thing with the what?"

"Nothing," he said, shaking his head. "Forget it."

"Because I thought you were going to mention the time I porked myself with some hot dogs at a party."

She didn't think it was possible, but his splotches got brighter.

"That actually might be my favorite of all, really," she went on. "I mean, how would that even work? Did I take the pack of franks to a bedroom so I could have some romantic time alone with them? Or did I just hop up on the kitchen counter and start going at it, right next to where people were doing keg stands and shit? Plus there's the nickname that goes with it. Oscar Mayer? Sheer brilliance."

She sighed.

"Anyway, that'll teach me to crash a Cool Kids party."

It hadn't even been her idea. For some reason, Molly thought it would be hilarious to go to a high school party, and Chloe just went along with it.

"It doesn't bother you that people say those things?"

Phillip asked. The spots on his cheeks had started to fade.

"I'm used to it," Chloe said with a shrug. "They're all losers anyway. Why should I care what they think?"

By the time they reached the other end of the trail, the sun was beginning to set. They'd found nothing.

"This is stupid," Chloe said. "Did we expect there to be a bunch of clowns just chilling out here in the woods? And we're just going to stumble upon them? We're idiots."

She turned around and started to head back the way they came.

"So that's it?" Phillip hurried to keep up with her. "We're just giving up?"

"There's nothing out here, man. Besides, it's gonna be dark soon. I guess we could try again tomorrow, but I don't know what we're looking for at this point."

They walked on in silence. A bird trilled from the tangle of branches above them. Under the canopy of the trees, it grew darker by the minute. Chloe felt like they were walking through a big leafy tunnel.

"Maybe we could set some kind of trap," Phillip said after several minutes.

"A clown trap?"

Phillip scratched the back of his head. "Well... yeah. I guess."

"And what?" Chloe asked. "We use some cotton candy as bait? Elephant ears? Circus peanuts?"

She started to laugh, and at first, Phillip thought she was making fun of him, being mean, but he realized then that she was right. The entire thing was silly. He started to chuckle too.

"We are a couple of nincompoops, aren't we?"

Chloe clapped his shoulder, laughing harder. "Total nincompoops."

# CHAPTER THIRTEEN

October 30th
6:44 PM

Annie didn't know that they could take her baby. The state. The Department of Child Services. She didn't know it was even possible until the social workers came and got him.

Now she stood on the roof of the apartment building, and she looked down at the ground four stories below. If there were a high enough bridge in town, she'd have gone that route. Better to jump into the river or into the ocean. Some body of water. The sea below this building was made of asphalt, but it would do the job. She was certain of that.

Time heals all wounds. That's what people said, but it wasn't true. Some wounds were fatal, and all of the time in the world made no difference.

She'd been making a grilled cheese sandwich when the knocks rattled the apartment door, and she knew right away that these weren't welcome knocks. In her experience, authority figures had a way of making their status known without saying a word. They broadcast it in their posture, in their walk, in their rapping upon peasant doors.

She cried after they'd gone, after they'd plucked him from his playpen. She cried and cried and cried, finding herself unable to stop. The sandwich burned, a black mess adhering to the frying pan, thick smoke crawling along the ceiling, stinking up the whole apartment, but it didn't matter. Nothing mattered.

She crushed up the six Vicodin she had and snorted the powder off of the back of the toilet in three fat lines. It didn't kill her pain. It just made it empty somehow, made all of her hollow for a little while. It didn't stop her tears. Only sleep could do that, it seemed, and it came in fits and starts. She didn't think she'd slept for more than 90 minutes straight through since it had happened.

Weeks went by, and it felt like she did nothing but cry and funnel crushed-up painkillers into her bloodstream by way of her nostrils. Anything she could get her hands on. Oxycontin. Percocet. Some muscle relaxer she couldn't remember the name of. If she knew how to plunge it straight into her veins through the tip of a needle, she would've done it. She would have pricked the inside of her elbows with great gusto, some remote part of her truly believing it might make the hurt go away, that if you were willing to go that far, to take the needle into your skin, that surely you'd be carried away from whatever troubled you by sheer force of desperation.

And maybe in some tiny way, the pain faded. It didn't leave her, but it felt a bit distant. Still present but no longer a smothering force.

She'd backed off a little as far as the pills, and she'd visited with her sister, staying a couple of nights at her house, eating home cooked meals. These things seemed to help. She still hurt most of the time, but it felt like something that could be endured, could be survived, could even end someday way down the road.

Today, however, she'd heard the news on the radio: some

**105**

lady's baby torn to bits near the woods outside of their apartment building. Shredded. A scene from a horror movie that played out just a couple of blocks from where she stood now. Maybe she could see it out there, the building, a set of lit windows shining in the dusk that she could identify if she knew which one to look for.

The story of the mutilated infant tore open her own wounds, brought the sharp edge back to the pain, twisted the blade in her heart. She could feel the empty place in her existence where her baby was supposed to be, a hole, a hole that would persist from now until the end of her life, a hole she could feel every waking second like a dry socket in the back of her mouth where a cracked molar had been wrenched out by the dentist's pliers, a void she could never stop prodding with her tongue, no matter how raw and painful it got, no matter how much it bled.

It was windy up here on top of the building, and with that October chill descending upon the city as the evening hit, the wind cut straight through the nightgown she wore. It stung at first, the cold gripping around the skinniest parts of her – neck and wrist and ankles – and spreading from there, the chill sinking deeper and deeper into the meat, into her bones. She was mostly numb now, though. The cold was a dull thing creeping into her core, making her bottom lip tremble.

She watched the city for a time, looking down upon the moving headlights and flitting shapes down there. Her tears changed speeds throughout this process as though shifting gears, slowing at times but never stopping fully.

She knew now that a person was never more alone than they are in the cold and quiet, when they are wounded and

**106**

exposed to the elements such as she was now. People stirred inside the building, just down one flight of stairs, no more than 50 or 100 feet on foot, but they may as well have been miles from here. She could not be more alone than this, more cold than this, more wounded and scared and inconsolable than this.

She climbed up onto the cement ledge, and the wind picked up just then so that her nightgown billowed around her. The cold seemed sharp again in that moment, the flash of pain blotting out her vision for a beat.

Her chest heaved with each breath, and she could picture the Earth rushing up at her, she could feel it, all things solid dropped out from under her and replaced with nothing – the plummet, the swan dive, the descent.

It was a long way down to the flat of the asphalt, the shining black surface, slicked with that little misting of rain they'd had earlier.

She closed her eyes, felt herself wobble a little as the air stirred around her. She tried to imagine what it would be like to hit the blacktop at full speed. She would break. Shatter. Crack open and spill her insides out like a beetle or some other insect with an exoskeleton.

Would she feel that, feel her skull fracture into little shards the size of fingernail clippings? For just a second, maybe, she thought, but the thought didn't scare her, really. The pain may be awful, but it would be momentary. The relief would last forever, wouldn't it?

She should try to land face down, she thought. It seemed that destruction was more certain that way. If she landed feet first, for example, she could merely snap her ankles and shatter her femurs, let those leg bones take the brunt of it and somehow live. That wouldn't do. Better to land face down and be sure.

Again the wind blew, moaning a little where it whipped along the sides of the building, swishing the branches around in the woods just off to her left, the treetops all swaying in unison. And the full force of the cold hit again, goose bumps pulling all of her skin taut, like in some tangible way her flesh itself was shrinking back from the chill.

She thought of her baby boy then, could see that far away look he'd had on his face when they took him away. He didn't cry, didn't seem terribly concerned at all. He'd looked a little serious, his eyebrows furrowed in a way that seemed to convey concentration, she thought, but that was the extent of it.

He was still out there somewhere. Would he have a new family already? A foster family, perhaps? She wasn't sure how it worked. The social workers had left stacks of paper, but she had been too upset to look at any of them.

He was out there, though. She knew that. He was safe.

Would news of this get to him? Not now, of course – he was just seven months old. But would he hear about this one day? That his biological mother was so distraught upon losing him that she jumped off of her apartment building and splatted in the parking lot?

Maybe. Maybe he would know about it.

She didn't like that.

What would that say to him about the world? That his mother was a drug addict who killed herself? What kind of a message was that?

She fidgeted now in a different way, her feet tottering, edging her away from the place where the concrete sheared off into nothing.

And despite the cold, the frigid wind cutting through her skin to chill her insides, she felt her heart beat faster in her chest. Faster and faster. It pounded with violence, teetering toward getting out of control. She felt the blood glugging along in the side of her neck, the vein there quaking with every thrust of her pulse.

She stepped down from the ledge and took a deep breath, and great warmth enveloped her like a hug. She didn't know where it came from, but it swelled in her torso, building to a tingle, and bolts of heat flared from there, shooting down the lengths of her arms and legs, smoothing out all of the goose bumps, withdrawing the numb from her fingers and toes.

The wind died just then, and the night got very still. It was all the way dark now and all the way quiet. Even as her heartbeat slowed, she could hear the thrum of her pulse in her ears.

She wouldn't kill herself. Not now. Not ever. She knew the pain, knew it as well as anyone could, but she would fight on. She promised herself that, promised her baby that.

Still, she crept close enough to the edge to look down upon that slab of asphalt shining down there. She needed, somehow, to touch the ground, to feel the pocked surface of the blacktop against her skin before this episode could have a sense of closure.

She left the roof and climbed down the four sets of stairs. Her feet clattered out a steady rhythm, each slap echoing back from the plain white walls and beige tiled floors here in the stairwell, the reverberations all piling up and fighting each other, all of them trying their best to mess up the timing.

She realized about halfway down that she wasn't crying. Not anymore. She wasn't sure when that had happened, but she was glad for it. She'd sleep after this, she knew. She'd sleep long and well for the first time in many weeks.

At the bottom of the steps, it felt strange to be on flat ground once more, to take steps that didn't lower her little by little. She padded across the landing and pushed through the big steel door, the bar handle cold against her palms. The swing of the door cut a rectangular hole into the building and she passed through it.

The chill hit her in the face as she moved through the threshold, but it was different down here than it had been up on top of the building. The wind was greatly diminished, and the air seemed heavier. Thicker. A motionless, dank density that swaddled all things.

She crossed the sidewalk and stepped down onto the blacktop. She'd done it.

She squatted to press both of her hands to the cold surface of the parking lot, feeling all of the swirls and dents and divots that comprised its rough texture. But that wasn't enough somehow, so she lowered her cheek to feel them there as well. In some distant part of her mind, she compared to this a traveler kissing the ground after a long, treacherous journey at sea.

The goose bumps rippled into place, starting along her arms and swelling from there over all of her, washing over her like a wave, every hair standing up straight and tall, pulling a little pimple of skin up with it.

# The Clowns

She stayed in that position, kneeling, her hands and cheek pressed to the blacktop, for a long reverent moment. It felt like she was exhaling the whole time, letting something go, even if she knew that wasn't possible. In any case, her body seemed to share in her desire to hold onto this moment, to let it linger. The goose bumps puckered on her skin for more than five minutes, she thought, tingling and roiling the whole time, prickling, almost itching. They faded after a while, and when they had receded to nothing, she sat up.

Her chest expanded and contracted, a pair of deep breaths hissing in and out, and she felt light now. She felt a great tension eased some. The sadness was still there if she checked for it, but the pain associated with it wasn't quite the same.

She stood, feeling just a little woozy as her legs straightened. A couple more deep breaths helped that go away.

And twigs snapped off to her left, out in the woods. She thought it might be an animal passing by, but the crunch advanced, seeming to multiply as it did so.

What the hell could that be?

This curiosity seemed at odds with another part of her, the voice deep down in her lizard brain telling her that now would be a great time to scurry some place and hide. Now. Now. Now.

She didn't obey the voice, though. Standing. Listening. Watching the gloom off to her left where the trees began, just faintly visible at the edge of the streetlight's glow.

The noises kept growing louder past the point of what seemed possible. Surely she should see whatever or whoever it was by now, but she didn't. It continued creeping closer somehow.

Finally, the foliage stirred. The tall grass swayed. The tree branches trembled.

A figure took shape in the darkness. It looked comically tall and skinny, skin and bones stretched to ridiculous proportions like a real-life Jack Skellington.

She caught herself. Why had she thought of it as an "it?" It was clearly a man, perhaps one with Marfan Syndrome or some similar ailment that would explain its lankiness.

It – he – picked his feet up high with each step, knees bending and lifting one after the other. He didn't seem in a particular hurry. It wasn't until he took those last few steps before exiting the woods that she caught sight of his shoes. Oversized clown shoes tromping at the brush. Perhaps those explained the high steps.

Still. Clown shoes? In the woods? That didn't make much sense. Her lizard brain raised its voice again: Run. Run. Run. Now.

She took a couple of steps back, reaching a hand out to touch the steel door that led back into the stairwell but staying in a position where she could still see the clown-shoed figure moving toward her. She had to see what was happening here, though it made her feel better to have a secured exit route at her fingertips.

As the figure trod over the grass field that led up to the parking lot, it stepped fully into the light. She could see the clown makeup decorating its face – black smudges around both eyes, an oval of red surrounding the mouth. It smiled along with the makeup, but its eyes were dead.

There she went again, thinking of the clown as an "it." She

considered this a moment as she looked into the dead eyes staring back into hers. No. She had been right in the first place. This thing wasn't a man. It was an it.

She slid her hand over the steel door without looking, lacing her fingers around the handle, hesitating. The clown was close now, just fifteen feet from her and closing the gap slowly.

More crashing erupted from the woods, and there wasn't so much buildup this time. Additional figures took shape in the darkness, clowns all of them, she thought, based on their silhouettes.

Yep. Time to go.

She yanked the door knob, and it clicked, not budging. She knew the sound – the spring bolt mashing into the strike plate. Locked. It automatically locked behind her. Part of her knew this, understood it, but the rest of her panicked, jiggling the handle, thrashing at the door as though that would unlock it, the steel door rattling in the frame.

She turned to run, but it was too late. A set of cold hands gripped her triceps, lifting her up onto her tiptoes with incredible strength. It ripped her around, swinging so she faced the opposite direction in a flash, and it moved a few paces in the direction of the woods, out toward the other clowns who now moved in the open area.

She kicked and flailed, and it slung her down to the hard surface of the parking lot, some wrestling throw that planted her hip in the blacktop, her temple crashing down onto the curb a fraction of a second later. Sight and sound cut out into silence and a bright white flash, and then her senses began a slow fade back in, all things muted and dulled at first, her brain seeming to reverberate inside of her cranium like a ringing bell, its vibrations somehow endless.

She squirmed over the asphalt, not sure which direction to move, not sure of anything other than that she needed to get away. Now. Now. Now. Her lizard brain was the only consciousness she had left, and she moved like a reptile for the moment, belly pressed to the ground, arms and legs scrabbling in a thoughtless retreat.

Her limbs still rotated as the hands plucked her from the ground, hands and legs clambering at the air, doing little digging motions, like a dog held above the water who falls into the doggie paddle pantomime out of instinct.

Two sets of cold hands grappled with her this time, dragging her out into the field just along the edge of the woods. The grass was all wet, slicked with condensation, and the soggy fabric of her nightgown clung to her body.

She blinked a few times and focused. The clowns stood over her like gloating linebackers who'd just concussed a slot receiver, hands on hips, feet just more than shoulder-width. They remained motionless for a moment. She was almost sure that they'd waited for her to see before they went through with it.

She was too numb to feel it when the first one, the skinny one, brought a blade to her midsection, and some part of her was thankful for the lack of feeling, for the strange detached way that she was experiencing all of this because of the head injury. The others began just after, clubbing and stabbing and opening her up.

She drifted in and out of consciousness as they dined upon the fleshy bits of her, some kind of shock removing her from the scene as often as it could and retracting her awareness fully into her mind, into the abstract. And she thought of her baby, and she was glad she hadn't done it, hadn't jumped. Even if it meant nothing, she was glad for the choice she made. He would know someday, and he would know the difference. She was sure of it.

The cold came upon her, much colder than she'd felt on the roof, cold enough that her bones ached throughout her body. And she was vaguely aware that the clowns had wandered off, returned to the woods, left her to die all alone.

The wounded places felt sticky, tacky with blood going gummy in the open air. And in some way it felt like a sweetness spread over her, the syrup hardening along the edges of the plate.

She felt no terror now that it was finally here. No pain. No existential worry about what it all meant, if it ever meant anything.

She drifted out into nothing. Her eyes glazed. Clouded. The muscles around them going limp, the skin sagging ever so faintly. There was a peace there in the final set of her eyes, even if a violent scene surrounded it.

She was gone, and all of her troubles and anxieties finally kept still along with her body.

Clouds flitted in front of the moon, and the field grew darker. She would no longer be visible from the apartment building windows, even as close as they were.

The night was so quiet. So empty.

After an extended stretch of motionlessness, the body convulsed a few times, ribcage expanding with jerks that seemed powerful enough to snap bones, arms shivering like sausage links on a skillet, and then the dead thing bent at the waist to sit up. It rocked a few times, diaphragm still flexing wildly to pop the chest in and out, the neck hunched down like that of a vulture, and then it began getting its legs around. It took a long while to get to its feet, its movements slow, lacking fine articulation and all sense of balance like someone who was terribly woozy. It wobbled for a moment, seeming to right itself some, and shambled off into the woods, giggling a little.

# CHAPTER FOURTEEN

October 30th
7:06 PM

As they retraced their steps, Phillip felt the faintest
sleepiness like sand in his eyes. It was dark now, he supposed,
even if it wasn't too late yet. Likewise, he figured having this
clown thing hanging over him of late had been stressful, and
now that they'd seemingly closed the case, he was ready to
rest.

They didn't talk much as they started back, the silence
between them having grown much more comfortable than it
would have been this afternoon. Phillip liked it, some sense of
wordless companionship that reminded him of what he'd
always imagined it'd be like to have a dog. His mom was
allergic, and they probably couldn't afford it anyway. He'd
stopped asking for one years ago. In any case, he basked in the
sensation now.

A good five minutes or more passed before Chloe spoke
up to break the spell.

"Here's a question," she said, and then she paused.

"What is it?" Phillip said.

"Did you say you were flunking social studies?"

"Yeah, probably. I mean, I'm definitely flunking geometry
– like, for sure – and social studies isn't looking great. At all.
Let's just put it that way."

"OK."

"Why do you ask?"

"Well, don't be offended, but I just… I thought you were a nerd."

"OK?" he said, the word trailing up at the end to make it clear it was a question.

"Well, nerds are supposed to get good grades and be all about school, you know? They're supposed to study all the time and get into Ivy League schools and all that stuff."

He mulled this over for a moment before he replied.

"Yeah, I guess that's true. I don't know. I guess I'm just a loser."

Chloe laughed at that, and it took Phillip a second to realize that she thought he had been making a joke. Maybe that was for the better, he thought.

They fell quiet again, Chloe's boots clopping out loud footsteps that seemed a little hypnotic. They didn't recapture that word-free affection from earlier, but they came close, at least in Phillip's view.

Maybe it was the way the shadows had expanded to shroud most everything around them in black, but the path seemed quite different going the other way. Somehow foreign. It looked different, yes, but more than that, it felt different. The atmosphere had shifted. Altered. Mutated. Phillip didn't notice it right away, too lost in the notion that they'd settled the clown thing – determining, in fact, that it wasn't a thing at all – but the unease crept up on him, seeping into his thoughts on some subconscious level until it overtook them. By the time he recognized it for what it was, he was quite uncomfortable. Quite scared, he hated to admit to himself.

Flippin' terrified were the words he conjured to describe it.

He glanced at Chloe out of the corner of his eye. She was a dark shape hovering to his left, her shoulders swaying in an effortless, almost liquid way that seemed fully disengaged from the ground, the pounding of her boots the only evidence that she was walking rather than floating. The frightened part of him knew that he should say something to her, but he was embarrassed.

He waited, clenched his jaw, willed the spooked feeling to pass.

A dog barked somewhere in the distance, and Phillip flinched a little, startled by the sound.

"Do you hear that?" Chloe said, stopping in her tracks.

"The dog?"

"Yeah. It's not right."

Phillip listened, really listened, to the dog again. She was right. It wasn't normal. The thing was going bananas, vacillating rapidly between warning growls and shrill screams, some awful blend of fear and aggression, all sheer animal panic. Even at a distance it made the hair on his arms stand up.

"Do you think… "

Phillip couldn't bring himself to say it, and Chloe apparently couldn't bring herself to answer him.

Crap.

They looked at each other for a long moment, just able to make out each other's eyes in the moonlight. She looked more scared than he could've imagined before this, even the black makeup caked around her eyes unable to hide the fear. He was sure he looked just as frightened, if not more. Neither of them spoke, both knowing what would happen next.

Chloe led the way. They left the asphalt trail, cutting a diagonal path through the woods, walking toward the awful sound.

The perils of navigating the woods in the dark slowed their pace considerably. Fallen trees crisscrossed the landscape, hellbent on snapping an ankle if they could. Random dips and holes in the ground seemed to harbor similar goals. On top of the dangers, the way was cluttered with branches and shrubs and all manner of foliage. They had to take it slow, Phillip knew, even if listening to the panicked dog warbling in the distance made his heart thud at a frantic tempo.

"How did we not think to bring weapons?" Chloe said. "Who brings fists to a clown fight?"

Phillip ducked under a pine bough before he answered.

"I think maybe before this it didn't quite seem real. Even if we both saw the clowns and kind of believed it, it didn't seem real until we were out here, you know? I mean, we still don't know what's happening, right? Not for sure."

Chloe shrugged.

"I'm pretty sure," she said. "As soon as I heard the dog, I was pretty sure."

As if on cue, the dog screamed, holding a shrill note for too long. The level of ferocity made it sound more like some jungle cat or maybe even a feral woman about to go berserk. Phillip never would have placed it as a dog without the context of the earlier barks.

The dog fell quiet after that, and Phillip feared it was too late for the poor beast, but the barking started up again after a beat. That was good. Mostly.

They were close now, the dog's screeching louder than ever, and the light swelled around them as they drew near to the lamps hanging over the street and parking lots just beyond the edge of the woods. Phillip listened for cars, but there were no sounds apart from those of the shrieking dog. Even the crickets that had accompanied them earlier on their walk had gone quiet.

The thicket here seemed to slow Chloe, her boots tangling in Virginia creeper, so Phillip crashed out in front of her, not out of heroism, he thought, so much as sheer dread. He needed to know. For better or worse, he needed to know what lay beyond these woods.

Nausea fluxed in his gut, and sweat clung to the flesh above his top lip, and his fingers flexed and unflexed repeatedly. All because he needed to know. He was sick with the need, smothered by it. It was funny how that worked. No matter how awful the truth might be, it was somehow worse to not know.

He high stepped the last few paces, letting his arms swing wildly at the branches that hung in his way. The heavy feet tromped down brush, grass swishing, branches snapping with pops as loud as broken bones. He didn't care how inconspicuous he was being. He cared only about knowing.

He passed the threshold and stepped into the clearing, stopping in the shock of the open air. Some strange agoraphobic panic came with this new sensation. His chest heaved. Dewy grass smeared at his feet.

The first thing he saw was the dog, crouching, baring its

teeth and working its jaw up and down as it fired off bursts of yelps. It was a beagle mix, he thought, its voice sounding bigger and deeper than the animal looked.

It stood by an old lady, the dog's master Phillip assumed. She had wispy gray hair, stooped shoulders and a terrified expression on her face. Figures surrounded the two of them. Figures that Phillip's eyes couldn't quite make sense of at first since they held so motionless.

Clowns.

Clowns with dead eyes and weapons dangling at their sides – knives, bats, an axe, a machete.

Nine of them.

Phillip's heart stopped. The whole world just stopped, held perfectly still for a long moment, and then the clowns lurched into motion, ready to attack.

Phillip went to yell, but Chloe appeared at his side, clamping a hand over his mouth.

"Are you crazy?" she said, words hissing through the tiniest crack between her teeth.

Before he could protest, the clowns struck. The bat whacked her skull, knocking her over, and the others descended upon the fallen body. She screamed. Twice. And then she was quiet. The beings writhed atop her, heads all bobbing and twisting. It looked like a pack of jackals stripping the meat from an antelope's bones.

"Oh, Jesus," Phillip breathed.

The dog managed to bite a forearm, tearing open one of the clowns, but then it was forced to retreat. It was too quick for the evil beings, looping away from them, trying to elude them while staying close to the old woman. The animal's screams grew more desperate as it evaded them, more confused and terrified.

"At least the dog is getting away," Chloe whispered.

But the dog couldn't resist. It circled in toward its fallen master, perhaps thinking it could still save the old woman. A smaller clown reached for it, and the dog struck, latching onto the wrist, clown flesh gripped in its teeth.

Another clown grabbed the dog by the throat, ripping it free from the wrist and slamming it spine-first to the ground with a sickening thud. The other clowns moved to the animal, enveloping it.

Chloe tried to say something but only a little choked sound came out.

Phillip had never witnessed such brutality, such cruelty.

"I think I'm going to be sick," he said, leaning over to vomit into the grass. It came pouring out for some time, a strange amber liquid that didn't seem to match what he'd had to eat.

After a second, Chloe pawed at his shoulder, something frantic in her touch. Phillip went to look at her, but another round of vomitous spray exited his mouth just then, distracting him. Foamier this time.

"Phillip," she said, her voice tight and small. She didn't sound like herself at all.

He glanced at her, finally, found her mouth wide open and her eyes open wider. He followed her gaze out to the grass field.

The smaller clown, the one the dog had bit, shambled in their direction, seeming to move faster now that Phillip had spotted him.

They ran, Phillip still dry-heaving a little. They trudged through the ivy at the edge of the woods, little vining pieces of plant roping around their ankles and slowing them. Phillip pulled out ahead, picking his feet up and falling forward in a wild lunge. The trees rushed past on each side of him, thick dark things whirring by like those orange construction barrels on the highway, and Chloe drifted farther and farther behind, her presence shrinking in his consciousness to something he was just vaguely aware of somewhere back there.

He cleared the ivy and moved into the cleared-out space under the thicker cluster of trees, a bed of dried out pine needles underfoot, soft like a plush carpet. Now he could really run, a full-out sprint, the light just enough for him to make out the deadfall he needed to hurdle.

The asphalt trail got within viewing distance, that slash of blacktop cutting through the woods. He stopped dead, breath heaving in and out of him. His chest felt wet inside, his lungs two bags of snail flesh in his chest, inflating and deflating over and over.

What the fudge was he doing? He'd left her. He'd just left Chloe back there to fend for herself.

Left her to the clowns.

He turned back, running faster this time. He didn't think about the dead trees in his path, didn't think about the dips and holes in the ground lying in wait to snap an ankle, didn't think about anything at all. He ran. His feet just knew where to go.

He saw her there, still fighting through the ivy, that small clown creeping closer behind her, somehow not struggling with the plant life despite the ridiculous shoes.

"Chloe!" he said without thought.

She was backlit, her features smudged in shadow, but he thought he saw relief flash on her face for a second. A flash of ice entered his bloodstream, some combination of excitement that she was still here and terror at how much danger they were both in.

He stopped, sucking great lungfuls of air, waiting for her to cover those last twenty yards between them, not sure what he'd do if the lead clown got close enough to be a real threat before she'd cleared the Virginia creeper. Hit it? He guessed that was all he could do, balling and unballing his fists subconsciously at his side.

He noticed that a handful of other clowns had entered the woods as well, though they were much further back. For now, they need only worry about escaping the leader.

She reached him, and he whirled to run alongside her, peeking over his shoulders to keep an eye on the one pursuing them. He thought he saw a glint of light from its open mouth, an almost metallic twinkle. What the hell could that be?

He didn't get time to ponder it. He tripped on the dead tree, his body flung forward, skidding into the pine needles and scraping up a big pile of them in a face-first slide, his arms pinned underneath him so his face took the brunt of it. He flopped like a fish to get his arms free and rolled over, his front smeared with the wet earth from beneath the needles.

"Get up," Chloe said, again her voice tight and small, totally out of character.

He scrambled to his feet, wiping pine needles from his face.

The clown hit him just as he stood, timing its diving tackle just right so that their heads knocked like two rams fighting over a mate. The contact laid him out and knocked him a little silly. He squirmed, confused, pinned down by the dead weight on top of him.

Sharp pain registered in that ball of muscle between the neck and shoulder, and he cried out for a second, but the hurt cut out as his hands got to the thing's throat and pushed it up, holding it away from him. All of these actions felt like things that were happening to him rather than things he was doing. He knew his hands were acting, but he didn't get any sense that he was making the decisions that guided them.

He stared at the painted face hovering above him, not really seeing it in his daze. He saw only the gnashing mouth, the teeth. Braces. It had braces. That's what had glinted in the light.

Chloe's boot entered his field of vision, connecting with the thing's chin with an incredible wallop. It toppled off of him into a limp heap, and she pulled him to his feet. He was vaguely aware of the other clowns crashing toward them, a thankfully distant sound, though he could see them in silhouette out there. He watched them a moment, looking to his left as he and Chloe swooped onto the paved trail. He knew he'd been knocked pretty loopy as he thought he saw the old lady among those chasing them.

"Are you OK?" she said, as they fled.

"I'm fine," he said. His voice sounded a little scratchy so he cleared his throat. "Just got my bell rung is all."

It sounded like what a gym teacher would say, he thought, trying to stave off worries of concussions and such. He could feel her eyes on him, sure they'd locked onto that aching spot just left of his neck, but she said nothing.

They ran as fast as they could, Chloe leading the way, and it was a while before he realized they were going the opposite direction of home.

# CHAPTER FIFTEEN

October 30th
7:44 PM

Chloe saw the glow of street lights ahead. Thank God. She didn't know how much farther she could go. She grabbed the sleeve of Phillip's jacket and hauled him off the trail. He still seemed shaken but kept insisting he was fine.

Their feet crashed through the overgrown weeds of an empty lot and then Chloe led them through an alley. If they could make it out to the street at the other end, they'd be right across from the squat. Once they got inside, Chloe thought they had just enough of a lead on their pursuers that they might be able to hide and call for help.

At the edge of the alley, she hesitated, worried that maybe the clowns had somehow surrounded them or gone a different route to cut them off. Maybe the whole city was already crawling with them. The street was empty, though, and she pulled Phillip up the rotting steps and through the front door of the squat.

The deadbolt groaned as she turned it. It had probably been years since anyone had bothered locking the door of this dump. She stood on her toes to peer through the glass, watching the street for any movement.

It was clear for the time being. Her hands patted wildly at her person, seeming almost disconnected from the rest of her.

When her fingers found the bulge in her pocket, they extracted the phone.

"What are you doing?" Phillip asked.

"Calling the police."

"Finally!"

Chloe held up a hand to silence him. The ringing on the line cut off.

"What's your emergency?" the 911 operator said.

Chloe's mouth opened, but no words came out. Instead she choked, coughing a little. Her eyes went wide. How the hell was she going to explain this?

"How can I help you?" the 911 operator said, the inflection of her voice growing a little more concerned.

"I need to report a murder," Chloe stammered, and Phillip nodded as if to encourage her. "I saw a murder."

"Where was this?"

"In the parking lot behind Park Terrace Apartments on Kendall Avenue. Well, next to the parking lot, I guess. In the grass. It was an old woman." Chloe felt like she was rambling now. Was she giving too many details? Not enough?

"And you're sure the victim is dead. Is she still bleeding?"

"I ran. But I'm pretty sure she was dead."

"How did this happen?"

Again Chloe's mouth didn't seem to want to cooperate.

"Clowns," she said finally. "People dressed as clowns killed her. With a... variety of weapons."

After a long pause, the 911 operator sighed, all of the tension leaving her voice.

"Please keep this line free for real emergencies."

"No! It really happened."

Another long pause.

"I'll send a patrol car by just to be sure, OK? Happy Halloween."

There was a click, and Chloe's phone blinked to indicate that the call had ended. Chloe stared at it for a few seconds without speaking.

"She hung up on me."

"Yeah. I get that a lot," Phillip said.

Chloe went back to the window, expecting to see the clowns closing in on the house from every angle, but the street and surrounding area still appeared to be empty.

"What is this place?" Phillip asked.

Chloe answered, distracted. "It's a house... what do you mean?"

"But people live here? So many code violations," he said, pointing to a notice stapled to the wall next to the door. "Building's condemned. Are you sure it's structurally sound?"

Finally Chloe turned from the window.

"Phillip, priorities! We are in the middle of fleeing from a band of evil, flesh-eating clowns. It's not the time to be concerned with the architectural integrity of the building." She glanced back outside. "Come on, I think we lost them for now, but I'm not leaving this house unarmed."

They moved deeper into the house. She was pleasantly surprised to note that there were lights on. Someone must have had the electricity turned back on. As they crossed the dining room, Phillip stopped suddenly.

"Do you smell that?"

He sniffed at the air and then whispered, "I think something terrible happened here."

"What?" Chloe said, shaking her head. "No, it always smells like that."

Chloe rifled through the drawers in the kitchen, hoping for knives and finding only a few sets of crusty, used plasticware and some spoons. She slammed a cabinet shut. Useless junkies.

"Who did you say lived here again?"

"My friend."

"Is your friend...?"

"It's called squatter's rights, Turdholder. This is all perfectly legal." The counter tops were littered with old takeout containers, empty bottles and cans, and a single ceramic coffee mug that someone had been using as an ashtray. Chloe lifted an empty beer bottle in each fist and handed one to Phillip.

"What is this for?"

"Clowns," she answered.

His eyes bounced from her to the bottle, as if he wasn't sure he wanted to touch anything that originated from this kitchen. She didn't blame him, to be honest.

"Look, it's the closest thing we have to a weapon at the moment," Chloe said. "If you wanna go back out there empty-handed, be my guest. But I'm not."

She held the bottle by the neck and gave it a test swing.

He raised an eyebrow but took the bottle offered to him.

"It's dual use, at least. If you get a chance, bash one of those freaks over the head with it first, then use the broken end to jab them in the eye."

Her fingernails clinked against the glass of the bottle, and an idea came to her. He *was* called Rick Dagger after all.

Maybe he had a knife or two or three stashed somewhere in his room. She hurried up the stairs with Phillip on her heels.

She lifted the thin mattress in Rick's room with the toe of her boot and kicked it away, hoping to find some kind of weapons stashed underneath. Instead she found a few porno mags and a smashed cigarette butt. Of course.

They went from room to room after that, searching for anything they could use to defend themselves.

"It's weird."

"What?"

"There are usually a bunch of people just camped out in here."

"In various states of inebriation, I assume."

She laughed. Maybe Turdholder was smarter than she gave him credit for.

In one of the bedrooms, next to a heap of dirty clothes and blankets, Chloe found a hammer. Not exactly a chainsaw or an Uzi, but it would do.

There was a loud thud from somewhere below, and they both froze, exchanging wide-eyed stares.

"What the fudge was that?" Phillip breathed, and Chloe put a finger to her lips.

They crept to the stairway and tried to peek over the banister to discover the source of the noise, but they saw nothing but empty hallway from their position.

Since Chloe had the hammer, she took point.

Her toe came down on the step first, then lowering the rest of the foot. One stair at a time.

A tickle formed in the back of her throat, and she tried to swallow to dislodge it. Her mouth was dry, and her tongue stuck to the roof of her mouth as if adhered there with some kind of glue.

Finally, they reached the bottom of the stairs. She could see through the dining room and into the kitchen from here, and they remained empty and motionless. There was only one room in the house they hadn't been in.

Moving a little faster now that they were on flat ground, Chloe skulked toward the living room.

With each breath her ribcage trembled.

As they moved closer, they heard more noises. Little scrapes and scuttles and pitter-patters. And over that, more consistent, a series of wet, sticky sounds. It made her picture a dog with a mouth full of peanut butter.

At the archway leading to the living room, Chloe paused, adjusting her grip on the hammer.

Flattening herself against the wall, she peered around the door frame and into the living room.

The clown had a single stripe of hair down the center of its otherwise shaved scalp. A clownhawk. The sleeves of its vivid clown attire were ragged and stained with blood.

It was bent over the recliner, feasting on the innards of... shit, it had to be Malcolm. The corpse's head was turned away from them, but it had to be him.

The clown was still unaware of their presence, wholly fixated on the gory buffet of entrails before it. Chloe knew she should take the opportunity to strike, that this was her chance to attack with some semblance of an advantage. But something about the clown troubled her. Its physique was somehow familiar. It was hunched over, and the clown suit bagged around its torso, but she could tell even so that it was tall and thin. And some element of the arms, the indentation where the deltoid met the bicep – and then she saw it. The tattoo. A skull with a top hat smoking a joint.

"Rick?" she said, without thinking.

The clown turned and snarled at them, and then it was on its feet, charging toward her with teeth bared.

The empty beer bottle rocketed out of Phillip's hand, a perfectly thrown arc that caught it square in the face. The bottle connected with the clown's skull with an oddly musical clunk before bouncing off, unbroken. It finally shattered when it hit the floor, but it had done nothing to slow the clown's progress, which lurched toward them unfazed.

# CHAPTER SIXTEEN

October 30th
8:05 PM

With an underhand swing like a softball pitch, Chloe brought the hammer up, catching Rick under the jaw with the sharp claw-end. The metal caught on the mandible, and Chloe ripped the hammer free again, taking a chunk of clown meat with it. Something oozed from the torn flesh, thicker and darker than blood.

His long, skinny arms flailed at her, fingers creeping over her body like something insectoid, catching in her hair and clothes. The frantic, fervent movements reminded her of the way he used to paw at her while they made out. One hand found her throat, spidery fingers encircling her fragile neck with ease. They started to squeeze, cutting off her air supply.

Phillip was shouting something and clinging to Rick's arm, trying to loosen the death grip on Chloe's neck. The scrawny frame belied Rick's strength, and despite both Chloe and Phillip struggling against him, he was pulling her closer. For a confused moment she thought he was trying to kiss her, but the drips of blood that ran down his chin and onto his chest were a reminder. He exposed his teeth in a sick grin, and though Chloe knew they were stained yellow from years of smoking, they stood out white against the red of the paint and blood smeared around his mouth.

**135**

Cranking her arm back behind her head, she propelled the hammer with all of her strength. The claw end grazed his cheek, cutting into the skin to reveal bone underneath. Rick's grasp tightened, and Chloe's vision blurred. Again she hurled the hammer, this time striking the temple. The crushing pressure on her larynx loosened, and Rick dropped to his knees.

When he let her go, she stumbled backward a few steps. But she wasn't finished. She got her balance back, and now she was the one advancing on him.

With both hands gripping the handle, she slammed the hammer into its forehead. There was a crunch as the ball end shattered the skull. As she pulled the hammer back to strike again, something warm spattered her face. This time there was a metallic click as it struck the cheekbone.

The battered clown toppled to the ground, and she crouched over him, bringing the hammer down on him over and over. The crunches turned to wet slaps as she turned his face to jelly.

She hefted the hammer, but a hand caught her wrist. She grit her teeth and turned, still on the attack, thinking the rest of the clowns had finally caught up to them. But it was only Phillip.

"I think that's probably enough."

Her chest heaved, lungs greedy for oxygen. She looked down at the dead clown. Blood and viscera pooled on the ratty carpet.

She supposed thrashing someone with a hammer was one way to end a relationship.

"So wait." Phillip's voice shook with adrenaline. "Your

friend was one of them?"

"I don't think that was him. I mean, it was, but-" Before she could elaborate, a voice rang out from the hallway. Chloe instinctively sprang to her feet and lifted the hammer.

"Holy shit! You killed Rick!"

The hammer in her hand drooped. Malcolm stood in the door frame, the grubby Hello Kitty blanket she remembered seeing in the clothes pile upstairs wrapped around his shoulders like a cape. Had he seriously slept through all of that?

"Malcolm, I know this is going to sound crazy, but that wasn't Rick. The city is being overrun by cannibal clowns."

Chloe expected shock. Disbelief. Maybe even laughter if he thought it was some kind of joke. Instead, he just nodded seriously.

"Ah, I get it. That makes sense."

Chloe and Phillip exchanged a look. Something nagged at Chloe.

"Hold on. If you're there," Chloe pointed at Malcolm, "then who is that?"

She gestured with the hammer in the general direction of the disemboweled corpse on the recliner.

"Oh shit," Malcolm said. "That's Tommy Dickface."

Phillip blinked. "Sorry, Tommy...?"

Chloe waved the hammer in the air, flinging bits of gore and spatters of blood off the end of it as she did so.

"It's just a stage name." She turned to Malcolm. "What band was he in?"

"He wasn't. He was just a total dickface."

Phillip cleared his throat.

"I'm still confused, though. This clown," he gestured at the mangled clown corpse on the floor, "was or was not your friend, Rick?"

Chloe blew a raspberry. "I don't know, man. That's definitely his horrible tattoo. No way were two people tasteless and/or drunk enough to get the same-"

A groan from the recliner interrupted her. All three heads whipped around.

"Aw, dude," Malcolm said, "Tommy's still alive!"

Phillip's eyes locked onto Chloe. "We have to get him to a hospital."

Stepping over the clown corpse on the floor, they shuffled around the recliner.

"You guys each take an arm," Chloe said. "I'll get his feet."

Phillip lifted one of Tommy's elbows. The hand flopped on the end of the wrist like a dead fish. He scooted closer, bending over the chair to get a better grip. The smell was horrible, a nauseating mixture of blood and poo. He was about to suggest they lay the guy on a blanket and drag him to the car when Tommy sat up. His mouth opened, and black vomit shot out from the back of his throat in a geyser. It hit Phillip in the face, coating him in thick goo that ran down from his cheeks to his chin and splattered onto his shirt below.

"Look at his face!" Chloe screamed, and despite the black tar partially obscuring his vision, Phillip could see the strange whiteness of his pallor. It was not the paleness of a cadaver, but the oily texture of greasepaint. Faintly visible around the lips was a big, over-the-top grin in red.

A choking sound gurgled from its mouth, and Phillip

dodged away from the chair, concerned he'd be doused again. Instead, it laughed. A rasping, phlegmy cackle that started low and steadily rose in pitch and volume.

"He's one of them," she said and swung the hammer. The face of the hammer connected with the skull with a sickening snap, a sound that reminded him of cracking eggs for an omelet. Almost immediately the laughing cut out and Tommy slumped back in the recliner, body gone still again. Phillip did not think he'd be having eggs of any kind for some time.

"OK, this makes no sense," Chloe said, and Phillip detected a note of panic in her voice. "What the hell is going on here? Did he look like that when we first came in here? Was his hair sort of reddish like that?"

Phillip squinted at the body in the chair. She was right. The hair did have an oddly artificial red hue.

"It's Zombie Rules, man," Malcolm said, as if this was some obvious thing they'd overlooked.

"Zombie Rules?" Phillip repeated and then spat black goo from his lips.

"You know, if you get bit, you turn into one of them. I bet Rick got attacked, and then the next thing you know, he's Bozo the Psycho. He takes a bite out of Tommy Dickface here and boom: now Tommy's one, too."

Phillip was still trying to wipe the tar-like puke from his face. He closed his eyes and ran a hand down his face like a squeegee.

Chloe massaged at her bruised throat with her free hand. "That would explain why I saw one clown the other night, and by the next morning, Phillip saw five. And there were way more than five in the woods just now... holy crap. It's the

139

fucking clown-pocalypse."

"So what do we do now?" Phillip asked.

Chloe tore her gaze from the grisly scene in the La-Z-Boy and swung her eyes up to meet his. "We get guns."

Phillip's lips parted, poised to tell her, but he said nothing. He'd been bitten in the scuffle in the woods, and he'd concealed it from her out of pride, he supposed, instinctively wanting to cover up his pain from her like a dog trying to disguise its limp. Finding out that the bite was a death sentence almost shocked him into telling her, but no. It was his weight to carry. Not hers. He'd see this out, eliminate the threat – himself included.

It was his civic duty.

# CHAPTER SEVENTEEN

October 30th
8:59 PM

At Chloe's house, Phillip stood in front of the bathroom
sink, the water roaring, spiraling out of the faucet and
slapping against that little chrome circle above the drain. He
cupped his hands under the stream, splashed a little cold
water in his face, and looked at himself in the mirror for a
long time.

Something about his reflection reminded him of a wet cat.
He was in a state so unnatural to every fiber of his being that
it seemed to make him physically smaller. More vulnerable.
More pathetic than usual, which was a feat in a way, he
thought. Something that hardly seemed possible before
tonight.

The little wound just next to his neck throbbed. He didn't
think it actually hurt that much, that it must be some mental
thing, knowing that the bite meant his end. It made him
sensitive to it, made him conscious of it at all times.

The shirt concealed the marks, the wet place where the
teeth had pierced his flesh. He peeled the collar back to look
at it one last time. Not much to see, ultimately. Not even
enough of a wound to make him bleed much. He brushed his
fingers directly at the tiny slits in his skin, prodding at them
until they stung for real and then sliding his collar back into

**141**

place.

He was going to die tonight. It didn't seem real, but it was.

His nostrils flared, and he smelled the potpourri that sat in a little ceramic bowl on the back of the toilet. The odor reminded him of peaches covering something foul.

He turned off the water, and the room felt very quiet, very lonesome. He hesitated for a moment in the bleak silence of the place, feeling the room progressively morph into something more and more eerie until it almost felt like this bathroom was a portal to somewhere else. Another world. Another dimension. He wished it was.

He thought of his mom, alone in her cell, and he was almost sadder for her than he was for himself. This bite was his death sentence, yes, but he wouldn't suffer long. She was doing life without parole in her tiny bedroom in their crappy apartment. Losing him would hurt her badly.

But he pushed the thought aside before the tears could fill his eyes. He had to. There was nothing to be done about it. He had more immediate concerns.

The door swung open, and he stepped into the hall, moving clear of that heaviness that mercifully seemed to hang back in the bathroom. He took a deep breath and joined the others.

"Why the glum look?" Chloe said as he walked into the kitchen. "You know you never really thanked me for saving your life back there, either. That little clown had you until I roundhouse kicked it in the throat."

She wiggled her eyebrows, some inside-joke type gesture that Phillip didn't understand.

"Yeah, thank you for that. Sorry," he said.

# The Clowns

Malcolm sat at the snack bar, two handguns and a pump-action shotgun on the counter before him along with a bowl of cereal. He shoveled a spoonful of Lucky Charms into his mouth, talking as he chewed.

"Lot of firepower here," he said.

"My dad seems to buy a gun a year, which is about as often as he goes out to the range to fire them," Chloe said.

"You guys think about calling the cops about all of this before you go in there guns blazing?" Malcolm said.

"I tried calling them," Phillip said. "They wouldn't listen."

"Same here. No one will believe us," Chloe said. "Watch this."

She cupped a hand to her mouth and yelled into the next room where the TV blared.

"Mom, we're going to be out late. Bunch of evil clowns creeping in the woods around here, and we've got to stalk through the forest and kill them all one by one. Don't wait up."

There was a pause.

"Very funny, Chloe," the voice in the next room said in a deadpan.

Chloe swept her hand in front of her, a gesture like a magician's assistant unveiling something on stage.

"See?" she said. "No one cares."

The voice in the next room spoke up again, its tone grave: "Wait. Oh my God."

"What is it?" Chloe said, the smug look wiped from her face.

"The stupid DVR didn't record Dr. Phil today. Piece of crap thing."

No one in the kitchen spoke. Chloe and Phillip just looked at each other. Malcolm refilled his cereal bowl with magically delicious marshmallows.

Phillip lifted the shotgun, feeling its heft in his hands. It was a Mossberg Persuader, a pump-action shotgun with a pistol grip. He liked it.

"I'll use this," he said. He scooped up handfuls of shells and loaded every pocket.

"Fine by me," Chloe said. She pulled a piece of Winterfresh from a foil wrapper and folded it onto her tongue.

"How long do you think it takes?" Phillip said, his mouth going dry as he spoke. "To turn, I mean. How long do you think it takes before someone turns after they get bit?"

"Probably depends on the severity of the wound," Malcolm said between bites of cereal. "Like Tommy Dickface went fast, you know, but he was all chewed up and shit. With a little wound – a single bite, you know – I bet it takes a few hours, at least."

"I saw the old lady," Chloe said. "The one with the dog. She was with the clowns chasing us through the woods. At the time, I thought I must be out of my mind. Anyway, that was pretty quick, right?"

Phillip's eyebrows scrunched up.

"I've been thinking," he said. "The one who... tackled me?"

He caught himself, almost saying "bit me."

"I think it was Greg Moffit. I mean, I know it was him. I saw his braces. He had these red rubber bands – still has them, I guess – and they're only on the top teeth. He wasn't in

**144**

school today, either."

Chloe's eyes went a little wide, and they all seemed lost in thought for a long moment. The kitchen clock seemed louder with every tick.

"We should go," she said, finally.

She had just placed her hand on the 9mm on the counter when a cacophony of shattering glass erupted from the living room. It sounded, in that moment, like a waterfall of glass shards breaking and raining onto the carpet, an endless flow of glass that just kept going. It was impossible.

And then the glass finally stopped, and everything was quiet.

"They're here," Phillip said.

They rushed into the living room to find a clown straddling the window sill, most of the way in. Chloe's mom looked dumbstruck on the couch, little exasperated clucks emitting from deep within her throat.

Phillip lifted the shotgun, his hand wavering. He hesitated for the briefest of moments, one tiny tick on the second hand of that kitchen clock, and squeezed the trigger.

The shotgun's barrel snorted and blazed, the orange flash filling the room which had previously been lit with the TV's glow. The report was an incredible boom that seemed to shake the foundation of reality itself.

The clown's chest ruptured, striped shirt and skin tattering away to reveal the shredded red tissue underneath, the stringy muscle fibers turned to savaged wads of raw meat, like a mess of those disgusting chips of steak in a fast food burrito. And the force seemed to eject the thing from the window, effortlessly thrusting it into the bushes outside before the bloody mist could even clear.

At the same time, the recoil nearly knocked Phillip over, wrenching his arm as though trying to fling him by it. It hurt, his shoulder aching as if the ligament was torn, but he stayed on his feet and got the weapon under control.

Everything went dead still for a beat, nobody even daring to breath.

"Mom," Chloe said.

Chloe's mom sat totally motionless on the couch, her lips parted. Her face looked more listless than shocked, Phillip thought, like mentally she was somewhere far away from here, totally incapable of processing what she'd just witnessed.

Chloe's tone turned harsh.

"Mom. Get in the bathroom and lock the door. Now."

The woman got to her feet, doing as she was told, eyes blinking in fast motion.

Smiling figures stirred outside the window.

"There are more out there," Phillip said in that gravelly tone just above a whisper. "A bunch of them."

# CHAPTER EIGHTEEN

October 30th
9:57 PM

Electricity thrummed through Edmund's veins as he sidled up to the car. Energy. Intensity. It filled his chest, tingled in his fingertips, throbbed in his face like a massage chair turned all the way up. It almost felt like taking a drug, he thought. Something that made him feel better than real life for a little while.

He'd watched the couple get out of the Volvo, cross the parking lot, and enter the apartment building. He'd watched them do this almost nightly for the past ten days. They parked here, usually between midnight and 1:30, usually heading inside for 15 to 25 minutes before returning to the vehicle.

Was it an affair? A prostitute and a john? Someone getting off work and changing clothes? Were they making a nightly delivery of some type? Something else?

He didn't know. He didn't care about the details. He cared only about the opportunity.

People making those quick stops – only running inside for a few minutes – those were the people who left their wallets and purses and tablets and laptops in the car. What were the chances, they probably told themselves, that someone would break into the car during that brief window of time? Those were the people he drove around looking for.

Trails where people went for jogs and walked dogs were
good, though it was risky to hit the same spots too often.
Better to find people like tonight's couple. People he could
blindside and never cross paths with again.

He slid the hooked piece of wire coat hanger out of his
pants and crammed it in that tiny gap between the window
and the door's innards, wiggling it all the way down. They
made tools for this, he knew, flat pieces of aluminum with
holes punched in them called slim jims for the police and
locksmiths, but he liked the coat hanger, liked the feel of the
little hooked piece gripping around the lever arm and pulling
it to disengage the lock.

The backs of his hands brushed the window, the glass cold
to the touch. The pressure of the wire bit a little into the
seams along the insides of his knuckles, but he could feel the
hook working its way into place. It was almost over now. Just
like that.

The lock lever jiggled on the other side of the glass,
working its way upward as he lifted the coat hanger.
Watching that little plastic nub rise seemed to double the
voltage of the electricity pulsating through him, turning it
cold, ice water vibrating up and down his limbs. His hands
shook from the adrenaline, and his heartbeat grew wild the
way it did during those first few thrusts of a sexual encounter.

The lever jerked the last little bit into its fully upright
position, and something deep within the door clicked. The car
was unlocked.

He pulled the hanger free of the door, cupped his fingers
under the door handle, and pulled it open. The dome light
snicked as it came on, the light spilling out into the street in a

little wedge shape that matched the opening, the brightness forcing his eyelids into squinted slits.

He got in and closed the door behind him, the leather seat cool against the clamminess of his back. He was sweaty. He hadn't realized it until now, though he wasn't surprised.

The wallet sat in the cup holder in the console between the bucket seats. He grabbed it, shoved it in the left front pocket of his jeans. He scanned the area for a purse to make it a matching his and hers set, but he didn't see one. He thought back, trying to remember if she was carrying a purse upon leaving the vehicle. He thought not.

He ran a hand under the driver's seat, finding only a wadded up Kleenex and various crumbs. Doing the same under the passenger seat unearthed a wad of fabric though. He pulled it free, revealing just what he'd been looking for – a lady's handbag, bulging with whatever goodies it contained.

The dome light clicked off, making him jump a little, his shoulder blades pressing back into that frigid leather. Jesus, he was jumpy tonight. That wasn't normal.

It didn't matter now, though. He was done.

He pressed the unlock button on his way out, each door clacking in unison to obey his command, every lever standing up straight and tall. He took a certain satisfaction in leaving the car fully unlocked, though he wasn't sure why. Did he want them to think that maybe they'd left it unlocked, that maybe they were to blame for what happened here? Or was it closer to the opposite: making his violation of their space somehow total and putting that on display? He couldn't decide.

Edmund didn't spend a lot of time examining himself,

didn't spend a lot of time analyzing anything. He lived for the moment and took the things he wanted. When he was nine and he wanted chocolate chip cookies and Gatorade from the snack bar in school, he took them. When he was twelve and he wanted bottles of Boone's Farm from the convenience store, he took them, pinning them into the waist band of his pants. When he was fourteen and he wanted the things he wanted from Britney Chambers in the woods behind her house, he took them, commanding her in a cruel voice that they both somehow knew she couldn't disobey.

Self-examination was a passing thought, a passing feeling, forgotten as soon as it happened, just like everything else in his life. The only thing he had patience for was thieving. Taking. He could wait like a spider at the edge of the web for as long as it took.

He tucked the purse up in his armpit and pinched it between his arm and ribcage the best he could, hoping it wouldn't be noticeable in the dingy path he'd walk under the streetlights out there. He stepped out of the shadows and onto the sidewalk. He'd parked just around the corner in a parking lot outside of an apartment complex, not wanting his car to be at all visible from what he knew would be the scene of the crime. It wasn't far, but he was shivering already. The night air was brutally cold against his sweat-soaked t-shirt, and he wished he'd worn a jacket.

Steam coiled out of his nostrils, and he could feel his armpit grip on the purse slipping a little. He had to resist the urge to fuss with it, hoping he could just get out of sight of the car as fast as possible. The corner looked so far away, let alone the parking lot and car he couldn't even see from here.

# The Clowns

A slight adjustment to his arm seemed to secure the purse, though, and something about that steeled his resolve. He was going to make it. No problems. He couldn't wait to go through the purse and wallet. He always waited like this. Grabbing them, taking them, and not going through them until he had driven away.

Tonight he'd be going through them at the Mobil station on Lovell Street. Before anyone had a chance to report any stolen credit or debit cards, he'd order just less than $25 worth of food from the McDonald's there – they sometimes asked for ID if you went over that. Then he'd drive across the street to the gas station – the one he knew for a fact had no security cameras – and fill up the tank. He'd sit in the lot and go through the purse and wallet. The electricity thrummed once more, liquid ice pumping through his circulatory system when he thought about it all. He was like a kid on Christmas morning. He could already taste the Double Quarter Pounder grease on his lips, feel the acidic zing of the Coca-cola washing it down his throat.

He crossed the street as soon as he got around the corner and out of sight of the unlocked Volvo, taking a diagonal path toward his destination and picking up to a light jog. When he stepped out of the streetlight's circle and moved into the wispy shadows of the parking lot, he knew it was over. He'd done it. Of course. For the first time during this ordeal, he smiled. The endorphins hit, quelling the pent up feeling, the restlessness, that the adrenaline had built up in him.

His car was in the back corner of the lot, just next to the little grass hill that sloped down into the woods. Out of the way. Inconspicuous. Between his euphoria and the lack of light, he almost didn't see the figures standing around the Grand Am until he was right on top of them.

The words spurted from his mouth before he could stop them:

"Holy shit."

He stutter-stepped backwards. They were clowns. Jesus. A bunch of clowns were leaned up against his car, and they stood up straight now that he was looking at them. He knew, on some level, that it was silly to be scared of clowns, but that didn't stop the hair on the back of his neck from pricking up.

The clowns moved toward him, all of them seeming to do so at once, though they didn't seem in a hurry for the moment.

Once more his heart pounded wildly like it did during sex, like it wanted nothing more than to tear its way out of his chest, but it was different than before. This time he was the one who would be violated.

When he saw that one of them had a knife with a long, curved blade, he screamed, his voice lifting into a falsetto after a moment.

He backpedaled again, the purse sliding out from under his armpit and spilling its contents onto the blacktop. Out of sheer panicked instinct, he stooped to gather it, and the clowns were on him.

A nightstick got him in the ribcage with a crack like a splintering popsicle stick, and he fell onto his knees, bent over to the injured side. A web of pain pulsed from the spot, and he clutched at it stupidly, making it hurt worse.

Some part of him made sense of it. They'd broken his rib. He screamed again.

# The Clowns

The nightstick's second stroke got him under the chin, catching enough of his throat to cut off his cry and knocking him flat on his back. The clown flopped down on top of him, pinning him down. He tried to fight, but it was so strong. It pinned one arm down and then the other.

His scream was a babble now. Nonsensical syllables strung together. His panic got so big that he experienced this in flashes, a sequence of events that he struggled to piece together, but he was aware on some level that the other clowns were here now. They were all around him.

Something big and sharp entered him near the groin, a stab thrusting up into his bladder, all of the nerves around his genitals screaming, and for a second all he could think was that the clown straddling him was mounting him like a woman somehow. But no. No. It was a blade. He'd been stabbed.

When they started biting, he wished for death with all of his being, his arms free now but thrashing without purpose, hands rubbing at makeup clad faces and colorful wigs, doing nothing to actually force them off or even deter them. He didn't fight them. He squirmed at them.

The shotgun blast was so close and so loud, the flash from the end of the barrel lighting up everything. He felt its incredible fury as much as he heard or saw it, a force that seemed capable of ripping a hole in this dimension.

The clown head hovering over him buckled and disappeared into a bloody mist. Chunks of blood and bone vomited down on him after a beat, their heat and consistency reminding him of chunky soup.

Clam chowder. Manhattan style.

The limp body flopped onto his, blood still surging out of the neck and jaw remnant in spurts to wash over his throat and chin. Some got into his mouth and made him gag. It tasted like rotten meat.

The shotgun pumped somewhere behind him, the clowns all looking that way, and he scrabbled back in a half-crab walk, his legs dragging along with him.

Phillip squeezed the trigger, and another clown face came apart before him. The Mossberg's recoil ripped into his shoulder, the gun trying its best to kick out of his hands. It hurt like hell, but it was fudging worth it.

The other clowns moved with urgency now, running for the woods. Phillip fired one shot after them, but the shotgun wasn't as much use at a distance, he knew. He heard Chloe squeeze off a few rounds to his left.

"Should we chase?" she said.

Phillip shook his head.

"Let's regroup and reload. They're quick in the woods, but we can catch them unprepared again. Better to keep them guessing anyhow."

Edmund sat up on the ground, breathing heavily. Wounds and bite marks covered the exposed skin of his arms and face, and blood seeped from his torso. His voice wavered when he spoke:

"I don't know who you are, but thank you so much for-"

Phillip pumped the shotgun and fired at point blank range, taking Edmund's head off above the jaw. The juicy spray flung everywhere, blood and brain and bits of skull, much of it spattering onto Phillip. A beat after the first wave of spray had settled, an intact flap of his scalp landed on the blacktop with a wet slap like a soggy wad of dough tossed and dropped at a pizza parlor.

Everything was quiet for a long moment.

"Jesus Christ, Burkholder," Chloe said. "That was cold."

"Guy got bit," Phillip said, his face expressionless. "He was already dead."

# CHAPTER NINETEEN

October 30th
10:44 PM

The Le Baron crept along the edge of the woods, all four windows down for better listening. They'd driven into the lots of three apartment complexes and a dentist's office which sat adjacent to the little strip of woods that cut through town. So far, they hadn't seen anything.

Phillip tried to keep the negative thoughts at bay. Part of him assumed the clowns were out there killing right now, growing their ranks while they drove around aimlessly. Another part of him focused on that little wound just above his collar bone, wondering how long he had left. His eyes maintained vigilance, though. They scanned the area, endlessly looking for any movement or other signs of clown activity no matter what thoughts tumbled through his head.

Something tinkled in the backseat, an unfamiliar noise with a bit of a sing-song quality.

Phillip wheeled to find Malcolm eating a bowl of cereal, the spoon clanging out little melodies against the ceramic bowl.

"How do you still have cereal?" he said.

Malcolm shrugged.

"I took a little nap while you guys were out doing your thing." He gestured with the bowl. "This is what's left."

He slurped at another spoonful.

"Isn't that, like, warm? And soggy as hell?" Chloe said, her eyes flicking to the mirror.

Another shrug.

"It's mush. But it's good. I mean, the marshmallows are still good, at least. Little blue moons and stuff."

Phillip turned to Chloe.

"Why did you let him come along, again?" he said, keeping his voice down.

"I thought you were the one who OK'd that?"

He shook his head, and Chloe rolled her eyes.

"Look, I'll stay out of your hair, guys," Malcolm said from the backseat. "By all means, focus on the clown thing."

"He's right," Chloe said. "I was just thinking. We've seen the clowns almost exclusively near the trail, right?"

"Right," Phillip said.

"So let's go to the trail. In the car."

Phillip's jaw clenched out of reflex. It was a hiking and biking trail, and signs were posted up and down it declaring that vehicles of any kind were forbidden. His mouth wanted to point this out, lip twitching. Twice. Three times. It made him so uptight, so uneasy, but...

"Ah, fudge it," he said, after a long pause. "Let's do it."

He watched Chloe place a cigarette between her lips, her lighter flicking to life and turning the tip of the paper tube bright red. For the first time in his life, he wondered what smoking was like, tried to imagine the feeling of smoke rushing into his lungs.

She whipped the car around in a U-turn then, and they sped toward the mouth of the little asphalt path. Clouds of dust kicked up around the car as they passed through the place where tires had worn the grass down to dirt by people parking at the trailhead.

And then they eased onto the path, the front tires lifting onto the asphalt lip and then the back, the front end just avoiding the yellow post meant to deter automobiles – a bollard he somehow knew this to be called. The reflective paint caught the headlights, making the post seem to glow. It felt funny to be driving here, the woods practically right on top of the car, and they took it slow at first.

Phillip swung the barrel of the shotgun out the window, finger at the ready on the trigger guard. He took a deep breath and exchanged a glance with Chloe, nodding that he was ready. They picked up speed until the car rocketed along, the driver's side teetering off of the asphalt and juddering on the bumpy dirt and rocks along the edge now and then since the trail was barely wide enough to accommodate a sedan. Some of the stones spat into the wheel wells and undercarriage, ping-ponging out strange tones like some Caribbean instrument.

Phillip adjusted his grip on the gun, staring into the gloom shrouding the woods. Part of him wanted her to go faster, making the prospect of catching the clowns totally unaware that much more likely. Another part of him was scared to death that they'd flatten some pedestrian out here, flying along like this on a footpath. It was a somewhat irrational fear given how late it was, but anything was possible.

No one spoke for a long while, and his focus on the task before them only intensified in the quiet. Cruelty had taken much from him in his life. It had beaten him and bloodied him and punched a hole in his heart, had hurt him until he felt worthless, but he had one last chance to strike back at it. He needed to make it count.

No one cared, it seemed sometimes. No one in the world. But he knew it wasn't true. He cared. Chloe cared. They would find the clowns, and they would kill them. And the world wouldn't reward their service. The universe would remain impartial. Uncaring. The people would barely even notice, but that was fine. They didn't care when he was alive. They wouldn't care when he died. He never expected them to.

He didn't take up this battle to preserve this fucked society. Maybe it was never about civic duty after all. It was something else, something they weren't teaching in social studies. He did it because he knew it was the right thing to do. That was enough.

The notion that he'd used a swear word in his thoughts didn't occur to him until after the fact. Oh well. It didn't matter anymore.

Nausea roiled in his gut, strangely cold and slimy like a pile of shelled oysters and clams thrashing into each other, weird wads of snot and pink muscles all writhing around in there. Was it just nerves, or was he spiraling toward his end? He didn't know.

But in a way, he was glad it would be over soon.

# CHAPTER TWENTY

October 30th
11:08 PM

The clown appeared in the middle of the trail, smiling madly, headlights reflecting off his moistened teeth and gums. Phillip recognized this one right away. It was the one who'd bit him. It was Moffit, those braces on his top teeth once more the telltale sign. He could see the resemblance beyond the braces some now, too, looking past the makeup at the shape of the eyes and jaw, the single eyebrow stretched beneath the forehead.

Chloe put all of her weight onto the pedal, the surge pulling Phillip back into his seat. He grimaced as he braced for impact.

The car bashed into the clown, tossing it out in front of them, an impossibly limp thing that arced back to the ground and skidded over the asphalt. There was a loud sound upon impact, a crunch, but the car was otherwise unfazed. Not slowing a bit. And seconds after Moffit's flight had turned into a slide, the wheels of the Le Baron finished him.

*THUMP-THUMP.*

They hit another clown then, this one immediately sucked under the tires to replay the sound.

*THUMP-THUMP.*

Phillip verified that the skull had been crushed in the

rearview. The neck shearing off into a flattened smudge of orange hair that made him think of a smashed jack-o'-lantern.

He turned around just in time to see a clown leap onto the hood of the car, arms wide, fingers hooked in the opening between the hood and the windshield. The smiling face hovered before them, its body blocking much of their view.

Phillip swiveled the shotgun inside the car, moving to shoot it through the windshield. The thing scrabbled up onto the roof like a spider. Its hands and feet clubbed at the metal, the roof buckling under them.

"Christ," Chloe said.

Phillip angled the gun out the window, firing blindly at the space just above the roof. He reeled it back in to pump it, the spent shell tumbling to the floor.

Chloe pointed her pistol at the ceiling and shot straight up, the gun blazing and popping, the bullets thwacking through the metal, the saggy fabric fluttering.

They held still for a beat.

"Did we get it?" Phillip whispered.

The thing lurched into Chloe's window, gripping the arm she had on the wheel, the car careening off to the left.

She slammed on the brakes, and they jostled forward in their seats as the Le Baron jerked to a stop. The clown gripped tighter around her arm, but inertia wasn't having it. He flew, tumbling end over end into the woods and splatting against a large maple tree. His head had busted open like a smashed melon.

And then the other clowns were there, just along the trail, turning to flee. They pulled up alongside one, and Phillip blasted it, the shotgun barrel flaming up, and the clown's back flapping open in red tatters, swinging wide on both sides like someone pulling open a pair of batwing doors that exposed his ribcage. The fallen thing held still for a moment, and then it lifted its chest from the bed of dead leaves and tried to crawl forward. It looked so wet, the heaving piece of meat sprawled out on the ground.

He wheeled and fired at another, this time blowing out the neck, the clown head swinging down, dangling as though hung from a string, which it pretty much was, Phillip thought. This one went totally slack upon landing, arms folding up under the torso in an awkward heap in the leaves, the most-of-the-way decapitation apparently finishing the job.

He pumped, aimed at another, fired. Head shot. A mist of blood and brains sprayed over the rear end of the car, and the thing buckled at the knees and went down. Phillip watched it in the red glow of the taillights. It didn't move.

"There are more now. A lot more," he said, as he shoved more shells into the magazine tube.

"How many, do you think?" Chloe said.

"Not sure. They mostly seem to be sticking together, at least."

He turned, trying to line up another shot, the clowns all running up a little slope away from them.

"End of the line," Chloe said.

Phillip glanced over to see the matching yellow bollard marking the trail's end. The car slowed, stopping just shy of the post. After a beat, she turned the key, and the LeBaron's rumble died all at once.

The first beat of silence was strange and somehow terrifying, almost unbearable, Phillip thought.

**162**

"Better to save gas, I guess," she said, and he was somehow certain that she spoke only to shatter the awful quiet.

Phillip squirmed in his seat. After a moment, he could hear the leaves crunching out there in the dark, the loud pop of the periodic twig snapping.

"Should we get out?" he said.

She hesitated, nodded, pursing her lips, the pistol rising out of the shadows, seeming to appear next to her face out of nowhere. Her index finger stroked lightly at the place where the barrel and stock met, the rest of her hand snaked around the grip.

"Malcolm," she said.

There was no response from the backseat.

"Is he…" Phillip said.

Chloe leaned back into the shadows, holding her breath as she patted around.

"Here," Phillip said. He opened his door, and the dome light flicked on, lighting everything up.

Malcolm lay in the backseat with that Hello Kitty blanket snuggled up to his chin, eyes closed. His chest rose and fell in slow motion.

"Useless junkies. He's sleeping," Chloe said. "What the hell?"

"Should we wake him up?"

Chloe shrugged.

"Let's just lock the car, I guess. He should be fine."

They rolled up their windows.

"OK, let's finish this," she said, and he could see those muscles along her jaw pull taut.

They stormed out of the car, Phillip waiting a beat until Chloe was at his side before moving out into the woods. They'd discussed the importance of staying together earlier, and it was never more crucial than now. Venturing into the shadows of the woods, friendly fire became a serious threat if they lost track of one another.

Chloe jogged over to put a bullet in the head of the one who'd gotten his back blown out. He had seemed immobile, but it was better safe than sorry when you're wiping out homicidal clowns like this, Phillip figured.

Again, they coordinated, positioning themselves shoulder to shoulder before they ran out into the dark.

Phillip stayed light on his feet, his ears focused on the sounds further out. Most of the footsteps seemed very far away, a stampede of thunderous crashes that sounded tiny from this distance. They'd be out of earshot soon, perhaps moving out of the woods altogether.

At least one clown was closer, though. It seemed slowed somehow.

Chloe held up her phone as a flashlight, sweeping it back and forth over the wooded terrain. Based on the way she did it, Phillip assumed that she heard the nearby clown as well and was looking to reveal it.

There it was, a hunched-over figure hobbling.

The old lady ran on a broken ankle, her foot bent at an angle damn near perpendicular to her leg, the jagged bones sticking out of both sides of the wound like toothpicks sticking out of an hors d'oeuvres. Even with her face painted, Phillip could tell it was the one they'd seen hours earlier, the one whose dog tried to save her.

**164**

She hissed at them, her tongue flicking out of her toothless mouth, seeming pointy and strange like a serpent's, though it may have been a trick of the shadows. When they closed to within point blank range, the thing lunged at Phillip, and Chloe shot it twice, the first hitting the clavicle, the second blowing out the back of the skull.

"Yikes," Phillip said, wiping more spatter from around his mouth.

Chloe looked out at the woods.

"I think I know where they're headed," she said.

# CHAPTER TWENTY ONE

October 31st
12:13 AM

"You were right," Phillip said, gesturing to an upper level window. "Look."

A clown glared down at them from behind the glass before stepping back into the gloom.

Chloe tucked her pistol into the back of her pants and unscrewed the spout on the red plastic gas can. For once she was actually thankful that her car was such a piece. Among other things, the gas gauge was broken, so she always kept a little spare gas in the trunk.

"Are you sure about this, though? Isn't this, uh... arson?" Phillip rubbed at the place where his neck and shoulder met. A nervous tic of his, she'd noticed.

"This place is practically asking to be set on fire. You said it yourself, Phillip. It's not structurally sound. Besides. It's Devil's Night. Do you know how many fires happen in this city the night before Halloween?"

She stepped closer to the ramshackle house, lifting the container to sprinkle gas around the perimeter, trying to splash the vertical surface of the outer walls. Gas slapped into the wood siding and dribbled down, turning the weathered grain a shade darker in the wet.

At the side of the house, she tossed a brick through a

window. Phillip boosted her up so she could soak the moldy and now bloodied recliner inside. She made sure to douse the entry points with extra gas, just in case. She held the can aloft, watching the golden liquid spatter and soak into the astroturf on the front stoop and a ragged welcome mat at the back of the house. She cough and gagged a little from the fumes.

"That should do it," she said, setting the can down in the grass.

Phillip cleared his throat.

"I just wanted to tell you that I, well... I think you're a pretty cool chick."

"Right back at ya, Burkholder. Well, not the chick part. You're a cool dude. Are you ready?"

Phillip nodded. Chloe pulled a pack of matches from her pocket. As she walked up the path of the house, she tore a match loose and folded the book closed. Exposing the strike strip on the back, she dragged the tip across. Just shy of the front door, she stopped, lit match raised in the air, poised to drop. Her fingers let go of the flaming stick, and she watched it tumble end over end toward the wavering fumes of gasoline. She didn't think it even hit the ground before there was a loud *WHOOMPF*! She squinted against the blinding light, and then a blast of hot air slammed into her, knocking her flat on her ass. At the same moment, the front door burst open.

A wave of clowns poured out, seeming to not care about the flames now engulfing the front of the house. She must have been a bit dazed from the explosion, so she just sat there. She watched the first go down under a shotgun blast, and that jarred something loose inside her. Her survival instinct. Her hands flailed around behind her, reaching for the gun tucked in her waistband, but it was too late. The clowns cascaded out of the house, quickly overtaking her, and then she was surrounded by a flaming mass of polka dots and ruffles and curly rainbow-colored hair.

They didn't seem to notice that they were on fire, and she wondered if they'd swarmed out of the house because of the flames, or because there was fresh meat standing in the front lawn. A white-gloved hand, spattered with fresh blood, wrapped around her ankle. She tucked her knee to her chest and kicked, her boot slamming into the clown's face and knocking it backward.

She managed finally to get her pistol free, and she shot at another clown that was scrabbling at her abdomen with its claws. She missed, striking the kneecap of a different clown in the writhing crowd surrounding her. The ear-deafening report of the shotgun rang out, and she saw one of the clowns go down.

The clown was pressing its face to her belly now, trying to rip through her clothing with its teeth to get at the tender flesh beneath. This time, she pressed the barrel of the gun directly to the clown's greasy white face and pulled the trigger. Its head exploded in a fine mist of skull fragments and brain matter. Chloe's eyelids pressed shut on reflex, and just then she felt a strange pressure on her thigh. She screamed as the teeth pierced the flesh, and somehow, though she made no attempt to avoid shooting herself, she managed to only strike the clown with a rapid fire *bam bam*! Two shots and the clown was dead.

A dark stain spread over the fiber of her pants, jagged

flaps of denim where the clown's teeth ripped through. But she didn't have time to mourn her mortality. There were more clowns to kill.

She scrambled backward and rose to her feet, taking stock of her surroundings. Some of the clowns had finally succumbed to the flames, lying in the grass in fiery heaps of flesh and polyester. It seemed impossible but still more spilled out of the house. She tried to take them out as they appeared on the threshold, gun cracking in a steady rhythm. But there were so *many*. Cascading out the front door and tumbling down the front steps, spewing from the lower level windows. She couldn't help but think of a clown car, and she chuckled.

The sound of her laughter was drowned out by another *whoompf*. A gust of hot wind buffeted her face as the recliner in the living room went up.

Her gun clicked, chambers empty.

Phillip took out two more with the shotgun, earning Chloe enough time to reload her pistol and start again.

One righted itself after Phillip blasted it in the gut. Its lower half was on fire, but still it kept moving. *Bam.*

Chloe put a bullet right between its eyes.

Another advanced on Phillip while he had his back turned, trying to line up a kill shot on a clown that was tangled up in the boxwoods next to the house.

*Bam.*

Dead.

The one she'd got in the knee earlier was dragging itself over the lawn, slithering almost, like something reptilian. Chloe hobbled after it, the wound in her thigh throbbing with each step. She aimed at the frizzy cloud of blue hair and pulled the trigger.

Breath puffed in and out of Chloe's lungs. She could feel the heat coming off of the house at her back, but steam still coiled out of her mouth with each exhale into the cold autumn air

The house was burning in earnest now, flames twisting up to the roof. Black smoke billowed out of the windows in a putrid cloud. What struck Chloe even more than the brightness of the blaze or the ripple of heat or even the choking smell was the sound. The roar was deafening, punctuated by sharp, percussive cracks and pops.

It was the only sound for a moment, the roiling of the fire the only movement.

"Did we get them all?" Phillip asked.

Chloe was about to answer when the noise of glass shattering interrupted her. A clown, completely consumed by fire, burst through a second-story window, landing with a crunch and a thump in the grass in front of them.

It lifted its head and shrieked. Without a word, and at precisely the same moment, they each silenced it with a gunshot.

They waited for more to come, and after what seemed like an eternity, Phillip spoke.

"I think we did it."

Chloe mustered a weak grin that quickly turned to a grimace when she put weight on her wounded leg. Phillip's eyes went immediately to the crescent-shaped gash on her leg.

"You got bit?"

Chloe nodded.

"Me too."

# CHAPTER TWENTY TWO

October 31st
12:37 AM

Chloe walked away from the blazing squat. Away from the stench of charbroiled clown. Away from the heat that prickled over her exposed skin and the smoke that stung her eyes.

She didn't know she had a destination until the spire of the rusty playground rocketship came into view.

The hushed sound of their feet on sand filled the night. Chloe fell back into one of the swings, gripping the chains with both hands. The metal was cold on her fingers, and she pulled the sleeves of her hoodie down to create a barrier between the chain and her skin. In the distance, a siren wailed.

"You know what we have to do, right?" Phillip said.

"Yeah," Chloe answered. She sighed, long and hard.

This was all a dream. Yeah, that was it. A nightmare. A very realistic – if you counted flesh-eating clowns as being realistic – nightmare. That spanned the course of several days. She'd had dreams like that before. Dreams that had a very real sense of time passing.

She remembered her psychology teacher saying that, though they often felt longer, dreams only really lasted a few minutes. Chloe wondered how that was possible. How could all of those feelings and conversations that sometimes seemed to span hours happen over the course of five minutes?

OK, so she was dreaming. Time to wake up. She pinched her tongue between her teeth, biting down until her eyes watered.

Wake up, wake up, WAKE UP.

She stopped before she drew blood. If pain was going to bring her out of the dream, then that clown taking a sloppy bite out of her leg would have done it.

No, this was no nightmare. This was real.

Tears formed in her eyes, this time out of anger instead of from the smoke. This was totally unfair. They'd saved the whole damn town from those psychos, after no one would listen to them. They were heroes, goddamnit. They weren't supposed to die.

And why should they kill themselves? To save the rest of humanity? Their townsfolk and peers? The people that teased them and spat on them and acted like they were dirt? They weren't worthy of that sacrifice. She wondered if her parents would even notice that she was gone.

How long did they have? She didn't know. She remembered one of them speculating that the length of time it took to turn depended on the severity of the bite. It struck her that the conversation would have taken place tonight, only a few hours ago. That seemed wrong. It seemed like days must have passed between then and now.

Maybe they were wrong. Maybe it wouldn't happen to them. She glanced over at Phillip swinging beside her. His face was smudged with soot and blood. She could just see the edge of the bite mark on his shoulder, the barest hint of scabbed over flesh. He'd been bitten hours ago and hadn't shown any sign of turning.

Maybe it was something that could be treated at a hospital. A new form of rabies or something. They'd get a few shots, maybe be kept for a few days of observation. She imagined them there, side by side in matching hospital gowns, watching bad daytime TV, and eating Jell-o off a TV tray like when she'd gotten her tonsils out.

But no. They'd seen it. With Rick and the old lady with the dog and Tommy Dickface. And this wasn't something that could be treated at a hospital. This was something that could only be treated with a sacrifice of flesh.

This was it, then. She'd never graduate. Never go to prom, as if she would go anyway. Never go to college. Never go to London or Japan or any of the other cool places she thought she might visit some day. Never fall in love. Never have kids. Never have another best friend.

The thing she resented most of all was that she'd never get out of this shitty town. She'd spent the last three years telling herself she would get away from this place. It was how she put up with all the bullshit. Endured the bullying and harassment. When she woke up in the morning and thought of another day in that school surrounded by people that loathed her, she would look in the mirror and say, "Hold on one more day." And then she'd think about getting in her car and driving up to the school, but instead of taking that left turn into the driveway, she'd just keep going. And she'd drive and drive until she was somewhere new. Somewhere no one knew her.

It had all been a lie, though. She was going to die here.

"Do we really have to do it, though? I mean, think about it. This whole town is just filled to the brim with jerkoffs. We don't owe them anything."

Phillip angled his face around the length of chain between them. "Of course we have to do it."

Would she feel it? She tried to imagine the change. Her hair going wiry. Her skin getting that pasty white texture that somehow looked both chalky and oily at the same time. She thought about the hunger. The craving that must drive them toward violence and bloodshed.

"I know," she said and sighed again. "It's our civic duty."

# CHAPTER TWENTY THREE

October 31st
1:12 AM

The fumes shimmered in the air around them like heat distortion blurring all things above the desert sand. Phillip liked the smell of gasoline, though, even if it bordered on smothering for the moment. He didn't know why. He'd never even driven a car or anything. Not once. It just smelled clean to him. Cleaner than almost anything in the world.

His eyes flushed with tears and his nostrils stung on the inside, the fuel burning the wet places on his face. He blinked rapidly, water draining from his eyes and trailing down his face, but he couldn't keep up with his tear ducts. He saw all things through that filter of water rushing to wet his irritated eyes. A blur that morphed and shifted constantly, his eyelids like fudged up windshield wipers that only moved the smudges around instead of removing them.

The hinges above squawked when he shuffled his feet to adjust his position in the swing, and little clouds of dust kicked up where he'd unearthed some dirt that hadn't been saturated with fuel. Not completely, anyway.

Chloe flicked her lighter, and he gasped as the flame burst from the shadow of her hand, but then he saw that she was lifting it to her face to light a cigarette. The fumes alone, apparently, weren't quite enough to ignite – a fact that relieved him, even if he would burn soon enough.

In the flashes of clarity after each blink he could see that water drained from Chloe's eyes as well, black makeup smearing down onto her cheeks. She looked so sad. She looked, in fact, like a sad clown. He almost laughed at that turn of phrase. Almost.

He wanted to tell her that they were doing the right thing. That he was sorry for it, but it was the only thing they could do. And that above that, he was thankful for how kind she'd been to him over the past few hours, even if it meant nothing in most ways. That he almost couldn't believe how kind she'd been.

Instead he said nothing.

She pulled the cigarette from her lips, turned the filter toward him and offered it to him. He took it, looking at the smoldering red end for a long moment before he brought the thing to his mouth and inhaled. The cherry flared brighter, and smoke swelled into his lungs, some strange thick feeling roiling in his chest, a sensation he found interesting, almost mysterious somehow. It tasted like dog shit. A thrill crept into his scalp as he exhaled, though, the hair follicles at the crown of his head tingling like mad.

He retracted the cigarette from his mouth, but he could tell by her body language that she didn't want it back.

She nodded at him and then gestured by flicking her head toward the ground. He knew what she meant.

Again he stared at the burning red tip of the cigarette, the smoke spiraling off it in slow motion. It shook just a little in his fingers. His carotid artery throbbed like a garden hose in his neck. He could feel its tremor in his jaw.

# The Clowns

He took a breath, almost gagging on the gas fumes.

With a flick of his wrist, the tobacco tube delivered that smoldering ember to the ground. Sparks burst everywhere as the cigarette hit cherry first, and there was an incredible whoosh as the flames erupted, the fire's great musk was everywhere, and then the brightest flash filled the empty space all around, engulfing them all at once in a fiery gust.

The fire trembled. It spat and fluttered and exhaled endlessly.

And it turned all in its grip to ash.

# CHAPTER TWENTY FOUR

October 31st
The Morning After

Police lights twirled over the grass, the red and blue shimmers reflecting back from all of those leafless trees that formed a kind of wall penning one of the many crime scenes in. Yellow police tape formed a more formal perimeter to match the natural barrier.

The police scuttled over the wreckage, spiraling around the dead bodies like carrion birds ever circling and circling until they found dead meat to sate their hunger. And there were bodies to be found. Many, many bodies. The forensics team would be working these cases for months, perhaps longer in some instances. Many of the dead were damaged beyond recognition, beyond hope for even dental identification. Even figuring out who these people were would be an incredible undertaking, let alone gazing into the smears of congealed blood on the ground and teasing out exactly what the hell had happened here.

It was a tremendous loss of life. A shock. An outrage the people of this city would talk about for years and years to come.

And yet life went on. The sun came up. The people rose and brewed coffee and went to work. The buses weaved crooked paths through the city streets to deliver children to school. It was like any other day in so many ways.

Even with all of the commotion, all of the trouble, all of the police streaming and scouring and cordoning off chunks of the city, Halloween proceeded, to some degree, as usual.

When the evening set in, trick-or-treaters came out in droves. They swarmed up and down the streets in clusters, filing along the sidewalks, clogging crosswalks, curling into cul-de-sacs, bounding up and down the stairs in the various apartment complexes.

Their bags grew fat with their hauls. Plastic wrapped chunks of chocolate. Wads of peanut butter candy clad in orange and black waxed paper. Individually wrapped fruit chews whose artificial flavors bore no resemblance to actual fruit or anything in nature at all. The least popular houses gave out apples and homemade popcorn balls that were somehow suspicious and off-putting in their lack of a sealed plastic sheath. The most popular houses gave out full-size Snickers bars in lieu of the much smaller fun size. An embarrassment of satisfaction.

This was the night when the sugar flowed like wine, when the nougat cups runneth over, when the little witches and ghouls reigned supreme.

And when the night went fully dark, fully black, the clown crept out of the woods to join the endless flow of costumed foot traffic, his smile swelling to fill his face, revealing the braces on those top front teeth. Nobody recoiled at his injuries or even noticed his limp. Not tonight. He fell in step with the teeming mass of humanity, totally undetectable from all the rest.

# ALSO FROM TIM MCBAIN & L.T. VARGUS

**The Scattered and the Dead series**

With 99.7% of the Earth's population dead and gone, the few who remain struggle to survive in an empty world. The scattered. The leftovers. These are their stories.

Keep reading for a preview of Book 1 in The Scattered and the Dead series.

# Rex

Panama City, Florida
68 days before

Rex ripped the IV needle out of his wrist, machines tattling on him with shrill whoops and cries. He didn't give a shit. He wasn't going to die in some hospital room by himself. Hermetically sealed in a plastic shrouded death box even though there were thousands of "ebola-like" cases in Florida alone, the number growing by the minute? No thanks.

He rose from the bed, his legs wobbling beneath him for a second. His vision swam along the edges, so he put a palm on the mattress to steady himself. He closed his eyes, took a few deep breaths. It seemed to get better.

Still, wobbling legs and dodgy vision comprised the least of his problems. His head felt like a swollen watermelon about to burst. It hurt like nothing else he'd felt in his life.

He was 43. He knew pain. This was un-fuckin-real.

Throw in the periodic projectile vomiting of thick, red blood, and you've got the makings of a serious problem. It was almost comical to have a doctor weigh in on this. Pretty straightforward diagnosis, he thought: You're fucked.

He knew he didn't have long, had known so for a while. In some ways, his fever rising to the point that his consciousness faded out into madness had been a mercy, had protected him from the worst of the suffering as he disconnected from reality.

But for the moment, at least, the fever had died down some,

and his thoughts were clear. He had a last meal in mind, a final resting place. It'd involve hard work, but his life had been full of that. It might as well end on a familiar note.

He prodded at the plastic sheeting cordoning off his bed from the rest of room, fingers searching for a flap or a slit or some opening to get to his things in the wardrobe. This wasn't a normal isolation room. Those were long full by the time he was admitted. Hospital workers employed plastic sheets here to convert this normal room into a quarantined one. He figured this was for the better anyhow as it increased the odds that his keys were still around. If he could find a way to get to the other side of this damn plastic anyway.

The only opening went toward the door of the room, the opposite direction of where he needed to go, but he guessed it would work well enough. He turned himself sideways, trying to make his barrel chest as svelte as he could. He sidled between the plastic and the wall, found the wardrobe, opened it. His hand fished around in the dark. There. His shorts, and in his pocket, the keys.

After a moment's hesitation, he slid the shorts on, but he didn't bother with the t-shirt, leaving the hospital robe to adorn his upper body. Fashion matters little to the dying, but he didn't like the idea of pressing his bare ass into the leather seat of his truck.

Hot leather pressed up against his sweaty taint? Fuck that noise.

He kept moving between the plastic and the wall, reaching the window and sliding it open. Here was the perk of being on the ground floor. He could pop out, cross a bed of flowers and some grass and be in the parking lot without passing a single nurse. The thought made him smile. If they knew, they would surely try to detain him under the guise of preventing the spread of the disease. What a joke that was. The world was already fucked. You weren't going to unfuck it by keeping him in a room with plastic sheeting for wallpaper. It didn't take Dr. Oz to diagnose that shit.

He dangled his legs out the window, lost his balance a little on the edge and tumbled down into the reddish mulch surrounding the flowers, his hands and knees jamming down into the wood chips. His head felt like swollen tectonic plates were crashing into each other just under the surface, threatening to rupture the shell of cranium surrounding them.

Everything went black and silent, and reality filtered down to only the pain. It just about knocked him out.

Un-fuckin-real.

Once the hurt passed, though, he chuckled. His hands retracted from the mulch, and he stood and brushed away the red bits clinging to his shins. The sunlight made him squint his eyes, but the heat and humidity wrapped themselves around him like a toasty blanket. He'd lived in Florida his whole life. This sticky, hot-as-balls air felt like coming home after all of that time in the air-conditioned plastic nightmare.

He staggered over the grass and into the parking area, his legs tottering under him, shaky and weak. No damn clue where his truck was, but he didn't mind looking around a bit. Being upright and ambulatory felt good as hell. The blacktop scorched his feet, but it didn't bother him. He'd walked over the hot sand on the beach since he was little.

After wandering up and down the rows, he spotted the truck and closed on it. If walking around felt good, opening the door and sitting down felt better. He was winded already, his head had that swelly feeling, and the world was just faintly blurry along the edges. Still, he made it.

Inside, the truck was stifling. This was beyond a toasty blanket. He liked the heat, but the sun beat down on the windshield all day. This was dog-killing hot. He started it up and put the air conditioner on.

And suddenly the victory of his escape seemed much smaller. His life would still end the same way: He would die alone, unable to visit his family for fear of infecting them, unable to walk more than a couple hundred feet without getting the brain bloat headaches or whatever the shit that was all about.

It wasn't supposed to go down like this. He'd planned for this, had a fallout shelter stocked to the brim with food and water and weapons. He had two bug-out vehicles. He had caches of supplies in strategic locations. He was a prepper, an intelligent and thorough one.

Unfortunately, the disease cared not. It killed without prejudice, whether you feared and respected it or doubted and ignored it.

He was supposed to make doomsday his bitch, and instead he was going to be among the first to go.

He reached into the glove box and pulled out a can of Skoal. It felt empty, but he was relieved to find a little left in there. He packed a wad into his lip, felt the nicotine tingle through the membrane and into his system. He leaned back and reveled in one of the few pleasures he could still enjoy. The final meal would come soon enough, but for now he would close his eyes and feel the tobacco in his lip and feel the stimulant enter his bloodstream and feel the temperature inside the truck return to something reasonable.

His thoughts drifted to his family. Maybe he would triumph over doomsday yet. Not by himself but by his kin.

His children were tough kids. His oldest, Ryan, got dared to go down a 25 foot ladder face first when he was 12. Rex came out of the house just in time to witness the disaster. Ryan fell, of course, banging his head on every rung on the way down. When the battered kid finally hit the bottom and stopped, he laughed. Everyone was frozen, mouths agape, certain that they'd just watched a 12 year old break his neck 6 or 7 separate times, and the kid fucking laughed about it.

His younger boy, Dylan, was a hell of a football player, too. Not the fastest kid, but one of those head-hunting safeties that just about decapitated any receiver that dared to go over the middle. If he were a step and a half faster, he might even be SEC material, but the coaches told him to expect to start hearing from the smaller schools as soon as his junior highlight reel got around.

His daughter, Mia, was the toughest of the lot. She was the bully of the family. Rex didn't know if it was a middle child thing, but she had a temper to her and had beaten up both of her brothers more than once, along with what seemed like half the kids at school. Personality-wise, she was the one that took after him the most.

These kids waded through some hard shit already. Their mother died of stomach cancer a few years ago, when they were still young. He was proud of the way they handled it. Not one of them bottled the pain up, they let it out, they lashed out, and in time they found ways to deal with it. They didn't get over it.

Rex didn't think you got over shit like that, nor were you supposed to. But they found their own ways to deal.

They'd be without their mom and dad now, but if they hunkered down and survived the first wave of this thing, those kids would be all right. He had no doubt of that. He wouldn't be leaving them high and dry. They had a mountain of food and guns and ammo thanks to his diligence.

Rex sat up and opened his eyes. He felt better. He plucked an empty Dew can from the cup holder and spit tobacco juice into it. Except what came out of his mouth was bright red and a little too thick. Almost gummy.

Shit.

He glanced into the rearview mirror to find red tears draining from his eyes. The scarlet rivers pouring down his face seemed to be gaining momentum.

Shit.

He looked away from his reflection. This was it. This was how it ended. He wouldn't get to eat that final burger after all.

He coughed and red spattered onto his fist. He felt the liquid churning in his gut, more of the same ready to come out the other end, he knew. As the flow increased to a gush, the blood filled his vision, turning it red then black.

He leaned his head back onto the head rest again, closed his eyes and felt the wet warmth of life spilling out of him. The fear crept over him now, made his torso quiver, made his breathing ragged. He hadn't been scared this way often in his life, but he was now. It reminded him of being a little boy, home alone in the dark.

And yet, he would die in his truck, not surrounded by his family but thinking of them. He could think of worse ways to go.

# THE SCATTERED AND THE DEAD

"All my friends are dead.
Everyone I've ever cared about is dead."

Want a free copy of The Scattered and the Dead (Book 0.5)?

For a free ebook copy of the prelude to The Scattered and the Dead series, please visit:

**http://LTVargus.com/get-scattered**

Book 0.5 and Book 1 can be read in any order.

# MORE BY TIM MCBAIN & L.T. VARGUS

**The Awake in the Dark series**

One second JEFF GROBNAGGER is standing in line at the grocery store, and the next he's in an alley where a hooded figure strangles him to death.

So that sucks.

This happens over and over again, every time Grobnagger has a seizure. Alley. Choking. Death. Repeat. What for? Why would anyone want to kill him repeatedly? Is it just a recurring seizure dream? When a sniper's bullet shatters his apartment window, he realizes two things: he's in serious danger, and there's no way he's getting his security deposit back.

Who is the hooded man? And who tried to kill Grobnagger in real life? His quest for answers leads to a missing girl, cults obsessed with astral projection, an arcane puzzle sphere, an evil book, a private detective named Louise and a mustached man named Glenn that makes the most delicious food he's ever tasted.

No one he meets is who they seem, and every answer leads to more questions, more seizures and more horrific deaths that may or may not be transpiring on some mysterious plane beyond the physical world.

The following is an excerpt from Fade to Black, Book 1 in the Awake in the Dark series.

# CHAPTER 1

Any minute now a hooded man will come barreling out of nowhere and kill me.

So that sucks.

I know this because it has happened six times before. I wake up in this alley, hung from a post by a piece of rope lashed to one ankle, tied in a hangman's knot. After several minutes of work, I pry my bonds free, and about thirty seconds after I hit the ground, this guy in a black hooded robe gives me a pretty bad case of death.

His hands are cold on my neck. And dry. I try to fight him, to claw at his eyes, but I can't reach. I scratch at his arms. He's too strong. I try to yell at him. I manage more of a gurgle and some clicky noises. I don't even know what I'd say, I guess, but I can assure you that he seems like a real dick.

Everything goes all fuzzy and fades to gray, then black. I die, and then I go… someplace else, I guess.

I don't know. I can't remember that part just now.

Anyway, I guess I should try something different this time. I fold at the waist, my fingers picking at the knot while I think it over. I've tried running out of both ends of the alley. Tried fighting the guy.

All of these failed in spectacular fashion. I'll need to get creative this time.

There's really only one other option I can think of. I get the knot loose enough to slip my ankle free of the rope and plummet to the ground, landing on my feet which immediately slide out from under me to plant my lower back in a mud puddle.

Nice.

I hop up and pop the lid of a dumpster open and lift myself so I'm sitting on the lip. Flies circle near my face before returning to their bacteria buffet. I totter forward, my hands latching onto the metal sides to stop my momentum. My chest heaves in and out with a single deep breath. This may not be the best idea I've ever had, I suppose, but I'd rather avoid getting strangled, so what the hell? I plunge feet first into the pile of trash. I sink and bags shift to flop their limp weight on top of me. Garbage water squishes around me.

It's juicy as hell in here, and it smells like liquid ass.

I can't see the soft mass resting under my hands and knees, but if I had to guess? Dead dog.

I never get a look at his face. The hooded man, I mean. He somehow tucks back into the shadow under the hood. I can make out the outline of his chin, one corner of his wet mouth, but that's it.

For now all I can make out is a little light streaming between the sacks of waste above me and the aforementioned juicy odor. I wait. And wait. I consider poking my head out to breathe some semi fresh air, but I decide against it. It'd be dumb to submerge myself in putrid liquid like this only to get strangled for trying to breathe oxygen that smells like 90% sewage instead of 300% sewage. I can tough it out.

After petting the dog for a few minutes, I hear footsteps rush into the alley and hesitate. This is it. I feel like I finally appreciate what the cliché "when the shit hits the fan" means, too, because in the dumpster it smells exactly like someone threw a bunch of logs into spinning blades.

The footsteps creep closer, and there's a sloshing sound. I picture his foot sinking ankle deep into a pothole turned mud puddle and almost laugh. Maybe I'm covered in piss and dead dog juice, but he has a wet foot now!

He scampers past the dumpster, pausing at the end of the alley before moving on.

Interesting. This is a new development in our game of cat and guy choking cat. As much as I want to get the eff out of this dumpster, I should wait here a moment longer before I move out. Give him some time to create some distance between us.

I stand, and my head emerges from the debris just enough to get a peek at the end of the alley.

Nothing.

I hold my breath and listen for a moment.

Nothing.

It suddenly strikes me that it really is nothing. No cars going by. No pedestrians around. This seems important, but I can't think of why just now.

I pull myself out of the dumpster, but my foot catches on the rim, and I splat face first on the asphalt.

"Fuck!" I say.

It occurs to me immediately that I've said this altogether too loudly considering I am trying to, you know, not get murdered. I bring my hand away from my cheek bone, and it's bloody with a bunch of sand stuck in it.

I look up, and there he is, standing at the end of the alley. Just standing there.

I try to think of a name or something to call him, but none of them seem dramatic enough to do this scenario justice. I mean, what can you say to the guy that's about 30 seconds away from snuffing your life out for the seventh damn time? Did I already mention that this guy is a real jerk?

I run. I reach the other end of the alley and bank to the left and keep going. My feet pound the pavement, and I can hear his footsteps echoing mine, drawing closer.

I take another sharp left at the intersection, hoping to gain a little ground with the change of direction.

For the first time I realize how gray everything seems. The sky. The buildings around me. The street. The sidewalk. It doesn't seem right. This place isn't normal. I try to remember what I was doing before I woke up in this alley, but I can't.

I cut left again at the next intersection, I guess out of habit at this point.

His footsteps are much louder now. Close. I sneak a peek over my shoulder just in time to see his outstretched hand reach for the back of my collar. I juke away from him and veer left. He follows, reaches out again.

Just as I think I should probably look where I'm going, I slam into the dumpster and drop to the ground like a bag of sand. I guess that's what four left turns gets you. My fall is so fast, he can't slow down in time and kicks my head, which sends him – Wait, let me rephrase that. I heroically place my head in the perfect spot to trip him, which sends him sprawling into the same mud puddle I fell in earlier.

I can literally see some stars from the cranium kick, but you should see the other guy. He's soaked!

I pull myself to my feet. I'm too wobbly to run, so I lean against the dumpster.

Aw, what the hell? I crawl back into the dumpster, face first this time. If this guy wants to kill me, fine, but let's just say he's probably going to have to touch a dead dog to do it.

I hear him move toward the trash bin, and then there's a familiar metallic sound that I can't quite place. After a very brief lull, I hear what sounds like him jabbing his hand into the garbage. He jabs again and then three more times in rapid succession.

Except I see his hand plunge through the garbage about three inches from the tip of my nose, and it's weird because his hand looks exactly like the blade of a ridiculous combat knife. Like if you had just killed a dinosaur, you would use this thing to skin it. Otherwise, it'd be too big to have any practical purpose I can think of.

So this is yet another new development. He's wielding a knife.

How wonderful.

I watch the knife jabs work their way away from me to the other end of the dumpster and then start their way back. I know I shouldn't move, that if I move he'll see exactly where I am. But once he's within about a foot and a half of me, I can no longer resist the urge to put the dead dog on top of me for protection. Before I can even lift the carcass, though, the knife skims my ear and enters that ball of muscle that connects the neck and shoulder.

This is the opposite of awesome.

He pulls the knife out, and without thinking about it, I lie back, I guess to shrink away from my attacker. I feel the wet warmth surge along the back of my neck. Things suddenly seem quiet, and I realize that I must have been screaming and just stopped.

The knife plunges through the trash once again, this time sinking into my torso two inches lower than my sternum, that soft space between the ribs. I grab his hands around the handle of the knife to try to hold the blade in so he can't keep at it, but he yanks it away without any real trouble.

The place where the knife was in my belly feels empty. A little cold. Like if you hold your mouth open and let the cool air touch everything in there, except a lot more painful.

I really need to figure out how I got here. Who just wakes up in alley that's all empty and shit? Hanging upside down by the foot? Someone must have put me here, I guess, but who? And why? And how do I even keep coming back? Who resurrects in this day and age?

I think I am in shock. Like now, I am out on the asphalt again. I guess he must have pulled me out of the dumpster. I don't know.

It's getting hard to keep my eyes open, and everything is a little blurry around the edges. I see the hooded man swing back into focus, and I realize that he's completely soaked. His robe looks like he's been rolling around in mud. It's a mess.

So that's good.

# COME PARTY WITH US

We're loners. Rebels. But much to our surprise, the most kickass part of writing has been connecting with our readers. From time to time, we send out newsletters with giveaways, special offers, and juicy details on new releases.

Sign up for our mailing list at:
**http://ltvargus.com/mailing-list**

# SPREAD THE WORD

Thank you for reading! We'd be very grateful if you could take a few minutes to review it on Amazon.com.

How grateful? Eternally. Even when we are old and dead and have turned into ghosts, we will be thinking fondly of you and your kind words. The most powerful way to bring our books to the attention of other people is through the honest reviews from readers like you.

# ABOUT THE AUTHORS

**Tim McBain** writes because life is short, and he wants to make something awesome before he dies. Additionally, he likes to move it, move it.

You can connect with Tim on Twitter at @realtimmcbain or via email at tim@timmcbain.com.

**L.T. Vargus** grew up in Hell, Michigan, which is a lot smaller, quieter, and less fiery than one might imagine. When not click-clacking away at the keyboard, she can be found sewing, fantasizing about food, and rotting her brain in front of the TV.

If you want to wax poetic about pizza or cats, you can contact L.T. (the L is for Lex) at ltvargus9@gmail.com or on Twitter @ltvargus.

**TimMcBain.com**
**LTVargus.com**